Touching Other Lives

Volume 2
Episodes 8-14

by

Margaret Gregory

TRIED & TRUSTED
INDIE PUBLISHING

Touching Other Lives

Volume 2
Episode List

Episode 8

More Clues to the past

Chapter 1

Once Martin and Annie had left the room, Wanda turned her attention back to Maude. "Okay, we only need to know recent things about Mickey at the moment. Since he came to get you this time."

Maude nodded.

"How do you know that the item he gave you wasn't his?"

Mickey Delaney did indeed consider Maude stupid. Too much so to be able to understand, recall or tell about the things he had boasted of or discussed in her hearing. This had been encouraged by Maude in the past, because of her difficultly communicating her thoughts through speech. She had also been aware that he could be dangerous if he was threatened.

With Wanda aware of her thoughts, she could ask simpler questions, which Maude could give short answers to, but those answers summarised the thoughts in her mind. The problem arose when the police officers wanted names of people Mickey dealt with frequently. That was solved by having Maude point to letters, hastily printed on spare paper. Her spelling was phonetic, but Wanda guessed each, and if right Maude nodded, and if wrong, she tried until she had it right.

When the officers indicated they had no further questions, they thanked Maude for her cooperation, nodded for Wanda to follow them, and strode from the room.

"How you handled her was amazing," one admitted. "How

do you think she would go in court?"

"Not well. She needs time to work out how to distil what she knows to be able to say it. I think any defence lawyer would have no patience, and tie her in knots."

"Let's hope we won't need her. In any case, she's given us ideas for new avenues to investigate to get corroborating information. How much longer will you be staying?"

"Depends on my superiors. If yours want David and I to hang around, they just have to ask. I do have some probably unrelated investigations I want to do before I go home. A few more days here at least."

"We'll be in touch."

Wanda returned to the interview room in time to hear Tyrell remark, "I wish all police interrogators were as considerate."

"Oh, I'm not a policeman," Wanda hastily admitted. "And we promised, no bullying policemen."

David spoke up. "My wife has trained in psychology. Once aware of Maude's difficulties, she worked out how to help her."

"Wanda good. She know my head busy."

"Really?" Tyrell remarked. "How did you determine that?"

"I did an evaluation last night," Wanda told him and then challenged, "Haven't you noticed that she understands what you say?"

"Well, yes. Though I usually don't throw in a lot of jargon. I just talk simply."

"Wanda ask me sums."

"How did you give her the answer?" Tyrell sounded incredulous.

Wanda collected the alphabet letters, to imply that as the method and not that she had read the answers in Maude's head.

"I'd like to try that," Tyrell said.

Maude nodded eagerly as if this was a fabulous new game.

"Can you give the answers by pointing at the numbers?"

Wanda asked Maude. She received another emphatic nod.

"David? Can you be the calculator to check the answers?"

Tyrell began as Wanda had with low numbers and working up to six figure numbers, calling them out at random.

After five minutes, he stopped. "Incredible! Astounding! Why didn't anyone ever discover this?"

"My guess is that they couldn't think of a way to communicate," Wanda said.

"She read my head," Maude announced. Tyrell looked from her to Wanda and said, neutrally, "So it seems."

Wanda winked at Maude, knowing the man didn't believe her.

"Gerald Hartley, Maude's eldest brother, could do sums like that. He was a walking computer. Charles, the second son, wasn't quite as good, but they both had a talent for maths. They went into investment banking. Too bad, they both died young, without children."

"I have girls," Maude reminded them. "Mickey said Gabby alive. He knows."

David added a warning. "Mickey may have said that to get you to come back to him and help him. I wouldn't trust anything he told you. I really hope that your girls are alive somewhere, but in a dozen years, no one has found them."

"I haven't stopped trying," Tyrell stated.

As they spoke, Wanda saw Kelly entering with the two teenagers. Annie looked pale, so she asked, "Have they finished with you two yet?"

"No, they still have to sign their statements. What about you?" Kelly countered.

"Same," Wanda confirmed. "Unless they will let us come back later. So what do you young things have planned for the rest of the day? When will you be back working for the scouts?"

"Tomorrow," Annie said.

"Well, I might just turn up. I hope you will come too, Maude."

"Not like place now," Maude said, sinking back into the chair.

"I understand, but I hoped to test how well you recall things from long ago," Wanda laid out the challenge.

"Do too well."

"So do I," Wanda admitted emphatically. "I don't like thinking back to when I was fifteen."

"What happened then?" Annie asked, wide eyed. Martin was also listening intently.

David said, "She was the brat from hell."

Annie nodded, recalling him say that the previous evening.

Wanda went on, "I ended up in a girl's training centre."

"Was it horrid?" There was sympathy in Annie's tone.

"The best thing about it was that I had a place to sleep and didn't have to steal for food."

Wanda met Martin's gaze, and he just nodded. He had avoided that potential future. Annie though was biting her lip. Wanda returned to the previous subject. "If we were with you, Maude, would you come? If there is anything else of yours there, I would rather you had it."

That caused Maude to look up. "Might find Mickey stuff. You have that."

"Sounds like a plan," Wanda announced, looking at Tyrell to see if he objected.

"I might just tag along," he decided.

"Baxter will try to put you to work," Martin warned.

The group, including the legal rep, were directed out by the retired CI Nathan Kelso. Wanda held back to talk to him.

"Can you find out when Maude's brothers died and the details? And her parents too, if you could?"

"Why? What importance is that?"

"Maybe none. It just might be interesting."

Wanda arranged with Baxter to take Maude to the scout house after finishing at police headquarters. Tyrell had already met the Scout leader, and now he was interested to see what had been done already, and hear what Baxter had planned for the following day. Martin and David opted to go with Baxter, while the rest went to check through the house again.

Annie led the way into the front room. "I found most of the things I showed you in here. Is this where you were sleeping?"

Maude nodded. "When girls gone, see them here."

"Memories?" Wanda prompted. Maude nodded, and in her head, she saw the little girls yet again.

"What about before then?" Wanda asked.

"Room at front."

Kelly held back until the women were in the first room off a passage. Part of the roof in that room was missing. Maude looked up.

"The ceiling collapsed between here and the lounge," Annie explained.

The room was sparsely furnished. A double bed frame with springs sagging, and a mildewy mattress and an old wardrobe with the doors hanging off were the main features.

"The bedding was foul," Annie said. "We didn't even want to try cleaning it. No one found anything in here."

Maude went to the wardrobe and swung the door around on the top hinge. It was empty, but she checked the two low drawers.

"No Mickey stuff."

While the others began to move out of the room, Wanda stayed back. Her eyes scanned the walls and floor and the still present part of the ceiling. She continued scanning, moving to study the floor. She surprised those watching her, when she went to a corner of the room and pulled up the carpet.

Annie went over to see what was under there, and was asked to hold the carpet up.

"What's there?" Maude asked.

"A sneaky floor hole," Wanda said.

"Probably another of Mickey's stash places," Annie suggested. "Somewhere else to stash stuff in a hurry if the police came calling."

"It didn't help him the last time," Kelly commented. "He was caught with the goods on him."

Wanda had pulled a slender lever like tool from a narrow pocket and inserted it into the gap between the floorboard and the wall. A cut out section of the board lifted up, hinged at the wall edge. A dank smell came up from it.

"The space under the house was searched," Kelly insisted. He watched Wanda kneel down and reach her arm in to feel around. She stopped moving, and concentrated on something. Finally, she pulled out a metal deed box by pulling on its wire handle.

She grinned at Kelly's expression. "From the feel of things, in this part of the house the ground is less than a foot off the dirt."

"Papa's box!" Maude said unexpectedly. "Lost it, Mickey said."

"Do you need a key?" Kelly asked Wanda, a grin telling her he was returning her unvoiced slur of the police missing finding it.

"No, I'm fine." She took something from another pocket, and used it on the fairly basic lock.

"What's that?" Kelly asked sharply.

"A hair pin!" she told him and Maude giggled.

When the lid was opened, folded papers were revealed.

"Why don't you pass it here?" Kelly suggested.

"Do you have gloves on?" Wanda challenged. She held her

hands up to show him that she did.

"There are some in the front room," Annie told him. Kelly strode out.

Wanda quickly rifled through the papers, checking random ones. One fell, and Annie grabbed it from the floor and instantly dropped it again. Her eyes had gone wide and she hardly seemed to be breathing. Wanda nudged her and she seemed to snap out of it. "Concentrate on breathing, kid."

The envelope, was memorised before Wanda put it back into the box.

"Do I need to worry?" Tyrell asked from the doorway, but nodded at the box.

"Probably not," Wanda told him. "Someone will need to look at these. And I am beginning to dislike Mickey Delaney more than just a little bit."

"How you guess it there?" Maude asked. "Never saw it."

"He may have rigged that after you left," Wanda told her. She handed the closed box to Kelly when he returned. "That may have some of Mickey's nasty secrets in." She reached out for Annie's hand and felt the girl was still trembling. "I wonder where else that vile man might have kept drugs."

"Bathroom?" Maude suggested.

"I hope you mean to look there, not that you need to go," Wanda said.

"It's okay. Naomi's dad had the water put on," Annie said.

"Look!" Maude said.

"Where should I try first?" Wanda asked after entering the bathroom. It had the bath along one wall, with a shelf at the head. Next to that, a washbasin with a cupboard under it and mirror above it. There had been a shower cubicle, but the glass around it had been removed, as had the shower head.

"Take that," Maude pointed to the mirror. It was mounted about an inch out of the wall.

Wanda felt around the edge, felt something move and opened the door of a built into the wall medicine cabinet. Inside were old neglected toothbrushes and squeezed toothpaste tubes.

"Take it," Wanda muttered to herself. Maude reached under it and snapped something open. Now Wanda was able to lift it up from the bottom, and when she looked, saw it was mounted on hooks.

"My sergeant will have our guts for dinner," Kelly swore. "We went right over this place, and now two women show us up."

Tyrell who had followed them silently said, "Be glad they're on your side, sonny."

"At least you have proof that Maude had a very good memory," Wanda took the opportunity to say. "You can look in there. You are taller than me."

Kelly did, and he reached in and brought out a collection of chemist's pill bottles. His face grew tight as he read the labels. Wanda reached for some he had put down and did the same, then looked inside those that rattled.

"I'd have them..." She began to say 'checked', but stopped herself. Kelly actually finished her sentence.

"I am beginning to see what my grandfather sees in you. Anything else?"

Annie tugged on Wanda's arm, and whispered in her ear, "Under the bath."

Wanda only nodded, and continued to look in other places. The cupboard only had a couple of thin towels, and when she took them out saw nothing suggestive of hiding places. She scanned the tiled floor, prodded any that looked uneven with her toe. Then she moved to tap the tiles that came halfway up the wall, jumping back when several dropped off. Seeing only the wall plaster behind them, she moved to check the tiles that were on the panel on the side of the bath. At one end, a lot of the tiles were loose, and more fell off. Not so at the other end. Wanda took out her lever tool and pried into various cracks.

She finally felt something move, and this time it was a tiled section of the panel that fell forward – revealing the space around the bath. Wanda put her hand in to feel around, and quickly pulled it out. She glanced at Kelly and he looked from her, to the exposed space and back. She shook her head slightly, and found a small torch in her pocket and tossed it to him.

"I'm sure you are capable of dealing with a spider's nest," she told him, to mislead everyone else. "We'll be back in the front room. I have some things I want to talk to Mr Tyrell about."

Chapter 3

"Is that all that was there?" Annie asked, sounding relieved.

"It's all I could see – cobwebs. Horrible things," Wanda gave a realistic shiver.

"I thought there might be another…" Annie shut up, realising she shouldn't mention the bones the police had found in front of Maude.

When they reached the front room, Annie gravitated towards Martin who was lounging against a wall, listening to an intense discussion between Baxter and David.

"Find anything?" Baxter asked, ending his conversation.

"Old paperwork, old medications," Wanda shrugged. "Might be something, might not. We do know Delaney was jailed for dealing drugs."

Maude began to walk through to the back of the house. At a mental suggestion from Wanda, David followed, suggesting to Baxter that they mention the plans that had been made for the house.

"Annie, you and I need to talk, When would be a good time?"

"We could walk home from here," Martin suggested.

"That will do for a start," Wanda agreed. Then she turned to Tyrell.

"I could say the same to you, Mrs Davis," Tyrell spoke first. "What is it that you have not been mentioning since we got here?"

Wanda gave him a faint grin. "Something I shouldn't be mentioning now either. They found remains of a young boy under the house. Now, I am not privy to what the local police think, but I do not believe Maude had anything to do with it. However, I thought that you should be aware of it."

"Yes, indeed. My thanks for that."

"That's not all, Sir," Annie blurted. She lowered her voice to just above a whisper. "I think, no, I know, that Mickey Delaney killed a little child in this place...in the bathroom."

"How can you..."Tyrell began, but he stopped, seeing a tight lipped Kelly enter the room.

"I wish I knew how you knew," Kelly said, looking at Wanda. "Maude knew of that cabinet, but not about the bath."

"I will explain more later. Let me just say that I have some talents that I am not meant to talk about. Are you going to call in a forensic team?"

"I will have to. Not that there was much I could see. I found some personal items."

Wanda sensed the truth of that, even though she had caught the edge of Annie's unasked for vision. She nodded to Kelly, then returned her attention to Tyrell.

"That box of papers we found today, I glanced at a couple. One paper appeared to be a POA, whereby Maude appointed Mickey Delaney to act for her. You will have to check with the police about that, but I would advise you to update all such documents, even if they are legitimate, and state that the new ones supersede any older ones. There was also a bank passbook. It might have been an older one of Maude's."

"I will look into that," Tyrell agreed, glancing at Kelly.

"And I think you should immediately ensure that if Mickey and Maude were ever legally married, that the marriage is dissolved."

"On that, I totally agree," Kelly added his personal belief. "She is better off without a user like him."

"You are both right," Tyrell agreed. "That demonstration this morning opened my eyes. I don't think anyone had ever challenged Maude's apparent intelligence."

"And I think Mickey Delaney assumed the same as everyone else," Kelly said. "I can hope she proves the one who helps put him away for good."

"Anything else?" Tyrell asked.

"Only that I wonder if there is anyone that can devise an IQ test that isn't stumped by her inability to verbalise her thoughts. I do believe, that since she has been living at that community house, she has improved. She has company, mental stimulation, and most importantly encouragement and respect," Wanda suggested.

"I intend to get a report on the medications that we found here," Kelly stated.

"Oh? And what would be the reason for that?" Tyrell asked.

Wanda answered. "While Maude was with Mickey this time, he claimed to have filled her scrip for her normal medications. One, how did he get the scrip? And two, what was in the bottles did not look like what the label said. In fact, they looked like some that we found here. More interesting, is that Maude told me she could think better when she didn't have them."

"I see. You have given me a great deal to think on," Tyrell admitted, nodding gravely in her direction. He saw Maude re-entering the room and didn't say any more.

Maude was smiling. She went straight to Tyrell. "Idea. Build new place. Here."

"Oh? You have already donated the house and land."

"House – bad place. Scouts good people. Keep little garden."

Wanda felt a distinct prickle from those extra senses that she didn't discuss. "What little garden?"

"One near tree. Buried now. My girls' garden."

"There are some old car wrecks back there and other junk," David explained from the doorway. "Baxter was telling me what he has lined up to get rid of the stuff. He has people who can recycle the stuff coming to get it and removing it for free."

"So what's happening now?" Martin asked.

Tyrell said, "I will get a taxi to take Maude back to the

community house. Unless she is needed for anything else.”

Kelly shook his head. “I will need to be here a little longer, to do a hand over. I have done a double shift and some. I’m past ready to sleep.”

Wanda grinned. “I guess I had better reassure Annie’s parents that she was never in any danger of being locked up. Come on! Lead the way.”

“Where are you staying?” Martin asked. “How will you get home?”

“With Kelso. He has hired a car for our use and David is itching to try driving on the wrong side of the road.”

“Is he allowed to?” Annie asked.

“He has an international licence.”

“I still have to wait a few months before I can start to drive,” Martin said. “Have to make do with a bike for now. My cousins have their driver’s licences, but at least their rich step daddy didn’t buy them cars.”

“Your cousins are idiots,” Annie said. “And speaking of idiots...”

Wanda eyed the two bikes approaching them and memorised the faces when they were close enough.

“Hey, Martin! Heard about your old man. Too bad they didn’t lock you up too. See you have a minder though.”

“You better be careful they don’t lock you up,” Martin called back. “You can keep Tory Michaelson company.”

Gerry Logan gave them a rude gesture.

Wanda turned to watch them ride on. “If they ask who I am, just imply I am a social worker. Misdirection. I don’t want my role here advertised.”

“It’s none of their business,” Martin said. “But I suppose, saying that will stop them inventing other ideas.”

“Exactly.”

Martin hurried his pace a bit, getting ahead and giving me privacy to talk to Wanda. I appreciated that, even though he knew what we would be talking about.

I had wanted someone to help me with this 'gift' I had. Right now, it was a curse and it was becoming horribly stronger.

"So what freaked you this morning with the baby shoes?" Wanda came out and asked.

It jolted my mind from the more recent vision. "You noticed."

"I did. You saw something when you held them."

I felt my eyes filling with tears. "Yes. I suddenly felt frightened and helpless. I saw a man, taking a child's shoes off. The child was screaming. I felt I was too. Just before I dropped the shoe, I had a flash of someone restraining Maude and stopping her going to the child."

"Did you hear sound?"

"No, it was more like an increase in pressure, and being unable to breathe."

"Have you had flashes involving Maude before?"

"Yes. That's why I wanted to help her."

"Tell me about them."

"I wrote down what I could remember," I told her, then mentioned what I had 'seen'. We were halfway home when I finished.

"That fits with what I know of Delaney. He has a temper. So, what was it back at the house? With the envelope?"

"I think it involved blackmail or something," I said, not wanting to recall that flash. "It made me feel I was about to be sick. Do you know how to stop that happening?"

"Maybe not stop it. I might be able to suggest some mind tricks to allow you to distance yourself from them."

"Please! Anything. I don't know what to do and my folks think I am just imagining things."

"I doubt they have ever experienced anything like what you have. So I am not surprised."

"But why can I do it? Is it some freak thing or genetic thing like me being good at maths like Dad?"

"I can't say, really. In my case, yes, what I can do ran in my mother's family. Anyway, what I started to do was hear what everyone around was thinking. You can't imagine the trivia that goes through people's minds that they never think anyone can hear."

"What did you do?"

"Well, I had David take me somewhere remote. I could still hear stuff, but not as much of it."

Martin dropped back to listen. "How's that like what Annie can do?"

"Ah, you are aware of that, are you? That's good, and it seems she trusts you. That can help."

"But what you did, how will that help her?" Martin persisted.

"Part of what Annie is receiving are emotions. The stronger they were when the article was imprinted, let us say, the clearer the images will be."

"Yes," I agreed. "Martin, you know when I jostled you, that day at school and you had that envelope..."

"Is that why you helped me?"

I nodded. "I knew you had nothing to do with it."

"Wish you could have seen why they did it!" Martin muttered. "But I am so glad you helped me."

I felt myself flushing. "So what can I do?"

"The first step is to be able to understand what emotions are yours. That existed before the psychometric impressions overwhelmed you. I want you to think of a really special moment and say a little mantra."

I listened and repeated the words she said until I had them

memorised, then I did as she had said. Maybe it worked, for my stomach stopped feeling like it wanted to empty itself. "What do those words mean?"

"I am not sure they mean anything. My mentor may have made them up."

"They sounded like some foreign language. So, what's next?"

"Next, is to find an analogy for how you experience the emotional aura. For me, with thoughts, I pictured a wall around me that blocked them all. However, there were times I wanted to hear the thoughts, so I added a door. I could change the thickness of the door so it would block different intensities of thoughts."

I considered the imagery. "That doesn't seem to fit."

"No, but it worked for me. I have a cousin who is a strong empath. She thinks of feeling emotions as like being in water."

"So, what does she picture?" Martin asked.

"I have never really asked," Wanda admitted. "I would imagine dry land as being equal to my solid wall, and being in various depths of water as the strength of the emotion I wanted to feel."

"It sounds so nebulous," Martin said.

"It's a mind trick that needs to be practiced until it becomes instinct. I expect that Annie does not wish to be caught like she was today."

"No!" I shivered, recalling what my mind had shown me. "I am not sure I ever want to see any more visions."

"Just remember, Annie, I am very glad you did," Martin said.

"Well, maybe sometimes. So how do I go about it? I mean, not everything I touch does that to me."

"Is it just touching things with your hands that does it?"

Wanda's question made me think. "No. And nothing happens if I have gloves on – like those you used at the house."

"Then that might be a better analogy. Practice focussing your mind to see yourself as wearing a skin tight rubber suit, and only your hands are uncovered. Believe that none of the sticky emotional residue can touch you anywhere else. Then, imagine yourself being able to have gloves of different fabrics or materials – from thick rubber, down to fine lace."

"Okay, then."

"At some point, you will achieve a balance. So you will just receive enough of the ambient effect to know if you want to know more. Then you can lighten the gloves further, or thicken them."

"So, I keep practicing that idea?" I wasn't sure if I did know how to do what she said.

"Try it, and let me know how you go."

Wanda took a couple of cards from yet another unexpected pocket. She gave me one and Martin another.

"I will get in touch with my cousin. Would you object if she contacted you by email? Erin might have more ideas that can help you."

"No, that would be great."

"How come you got so involved with Maude," Martin asked Wanda.

"Why did you?" she challenged him.

"Because of me," I admitted. "From that first time at the scout house. You know, when I saw or sensed her cowering from a man brandishing a saucepan. I learnt that she'd had an accident and lost her children. It just wasn't fair."

"Life isn't always fair," Wanda mused aloud. "But I am of the opinion that some things happen for a reason. Like your gift becoming stronger. Like detective Kelly's grandfather bringing me here, and my superiors actually agreeing. When I met Maude, I felt there was something I should be doing."

"Well, you helped catch Delaney," Martin pointed out.

"A violent piece of trash who won't talk," Wanda countered. "What that tells me is that there is something else going on that he thinks silence will benefit him."

"Does he really matter?" I asked. "If he is in jail, what can he do? I mean, you got that thing he stole back."

"His role in that was opportunistic. He and his accomplices robbed a truck full of electrical goods, it just happened that the original thieves were using that truck to transport the unit. Or, he might have been hired to target that truck. Like I said, he isn't talking. He was an acceptable scapegoat if something went wrong. There were two groups after him last night, besides the task force. Anyway, I expect he accepted payment for all sorts of dirty work."

"But none of that has anything to do with us," I hoped.

"I hope not, but he might have done things that affects other people too, not just Maude."

"You mean, like he killed a guard and that affects the guard's family," Martin put it in words. "If my old man was involved in that, then I hope I never have to see him again. Do you know anything about him?"

"Not a lot. I am not exactly privy to all the enquiries related to that robbery. In fact, David and I should really be heading back home, leaving the clean up to the local police."

"I wish you could stay longer," I admitted. "What if what you suggested doesn't work?"

"Keep at it. It is like an exercise to build muscles. And email me if you want."

"Will you still be coming to the house tomorrow?" Martin asked.

"Was intending to. It was the Hartley Family trust that donated the property. What do you think of Maude's idea to pull the place down and rebuild it?"

"Brilliant," Martin said.

I agreed, but I was reminded that Maude's maiden name was Hartley, and of the birth certificate Abbie had found. I still wasn't sure if I should mention that.

It was after lunch before I left to help at the house. Mum insisted that I finished the homework that was due tomorrow. I had warned Martin, and he was waiting for me at the corner of his street. Lucky-pup was up to her usual trick of sniffing at everything. She had let me know that she'd missed me yesterday, and I felt bad at the thought of leaving her at home by herself again. Mum was at work, and Dad had gone out early and would probably be at the house by now.

"I assume that the police haven't taken over the house again since I haven't heard that this working bee is off," Martin greeted me.

"I wonder what the police made of whatever they found," I commented.

"Maybe enough so that they can close an old case. They won't tell us anything anyway."

"Perhaps it will be in the papers."

"Yeah, and add to the rumours about the scout house. They should write a book about the place. It's getting notorious."

We reached the milk bar, and didn't see anyone hanging around. Maybe the Logans and the Hells Angels had finally heeded the warnings they'd had, or the activity down the road had caught their attention. Half the road was blocked off, and a crane was lifting the chassis of a wrecked car over the house and swinging it around to a truck with a long flatbed tray. A police car was parked nearby, and the officers were keeping the spectators well out of the way.

"Maybe they won't let us in," Martin suggested.

"I'll call Naomi!"

As we got closer, we saw some old whitegoods in a large

trailer, and a skip for other miscellaneous rubbish. We waited until after the car had been dropped on the tray, and the chains from the crane were headed away.

"Hey, Martin!" Gerry Logan called. He had stopped his bike behind us.

"Ignore him," Martin said, nudging me to cross the road.

"Got a great car for you," Gerry persisted, riding slowly after us.

"For me? I can't drive for two or three years yet. You'd best grab it while you can. Get Tory Michaelson to do it up for you. Have you seen that Monaro of his? It's fantastic."

Martin hadn't given him a chance to butt in, and he didn't reply immediately. He murmured to me, "He can't make up his mind which insult to reply to."

"Obviously, you haven't heard yet?"

"Heard what? That you finally saw sense?"

"No, ignoramus! The cops took the car off him. They reckon it's not roadworthy."

"Huh! What a surprise. It was rather noisy. Will they let him have it back?"

"I doubt it. They reckon it was done up with drug money, and is the proceeds of a crime."

"Well, then, maybe you can buy it cheap at a police auction. Anyway, was that idiot carrying stuff?"

Martin turned to see Gerry nodding. He wasn't looking so cocky arrogant now. "Hey, you and Tom weren't implicated were you?"

"Nah! Just asked if we knew about him dealing."

"And naturally, you didn't." Martin just shook his head. "How about you come with us and do some useful work?"

Now Gerry laughed. "Not me! You should drag that old girlfriend of yours to help. She's got to do community service. Deserves worse for getting Adam in trouble. Probably dobbed Tory in too."

I wanted to blurt out that Tory had got what he deserved, but

Lucky-pup chose that moment to start pulling on her lead. I saw Naomi waving us in.

"Leave the lazy sod," Martin advised.

I glanced back and saw Gerry eyeing us both.

"Now you have the house to yourself, Cuz, maybe we can bring some beer over, huh?"

"No, you're not meant to associate with me, remember? Step-daddy wouldn't like it."

Gerry growled rude words, as we headed towards Naomi.

"How long have they been at this?" I asked her.

"Since about nine. We got sent around to the neighbours yesterday to warn about the noise. They shouldn't have that much more to do. The rest of the scouts are coming at two."

"Have you found anything unexpected?" Martin asked.

"Dad was on about watching out for snakes, but I didn't think there'd be any of those around."

"I meant stuff that someone tried to hide."

"Oh. No, I don't think so. The police bought in a sniffer dog. It checks all the rusty junk before it gets lifted."

"So, what can we do?" I asked. I didn't want to think about things that had already been found here.

"We can start working inside, if we keep to the end of the house furthest from the crane. Some American woman has just finished going over the roof. She found a lot of cracked tiles, mostly over where the roof collapsed. Dad said something about checking the timbers in the roof. He mentioned something about seeing your dad for a costing for demolishing this place and rebuilding it."

"Yeah, I know. Maude Delaney suggested it."

"Were you here yesterday too?"

"Yes. Long story, but Martin and I found Maude on Friday, and she stayed at my place that night."

"Really? Tell me all!"

"If you two are going to gossip, I'll take the pup out of the way. I want to see how the back yard looks."

"Don't let her get loose. She might get stepped on," I said.

"Or gobbled by the police dog," Naomi warned, then grinned. "Though Rufus is a perfect gentleman."

I followed Naomi to the laundry, where I saw a ladder below an open man-hole. I couldn't help glancing sideways into the bathroom. It didn't look like a crime scene.

"I was about to start cleaning out junk from in here," Naomi told me. "The cupboards are icky. That three door one is full of old towels, going into holes. The ones under the sink have all sorts of cleaning stuff, with the labels chewed or decayed off. And piles of old papers."

"All where kids could get to it?"

"No, actually. They had those plastic kid proof things on them. I'm surprised no one ripped them off."

While we opened up some big plastic bags, we started hearing noises coming from the roof. While we stared upwards, a pair of legs in close fitting track pants appeared, and dangled above the top ladder step, gradually getting lower, and then the person's body appeared as the feet descended the ladder steps.

"Hi, Annie."

I should have guessed it would be her, or her husband. "Hi! What's it like up there?"

Considering that her dark outfit was dusty and had cobwebs adhering to it, I was glad no one asked me to go up there.

"I have scared off the nesting birds, although they may have been long gone anyway, and had a discussion with a couple of possums. Rude critters, but then I don't think they would want to go outside with all the goings on out there."

Wanda perched on the top of the ladder.

"Possums are nocturnal," Naomi told her. "We might be able to get someone from the council to get them."

"Aren't they protected?" I asked.

"Well if your local dog catchers have a long pole with a loop at the end, I'll get them out," Wanda offered. "I don't think you will want to keep them as tenants."

Hearing voices, Baxter bustled in. "Any sign of asbestos up there?"

"First thing I checked," she assured him. "I take it that the police didn't search up there?"

That caused him to stop and stare at her. "No, why?"

"People sometimes hide valuables in their roof."

"Find anything?"

"No. But I need a better torch and a broom or something to remove cobwebs, bird nests and possum droppings and to keep some rude little critters away. I didn't go in very far, so I don't know where they got in. Probably through the eaves."

"Want us to check?" Naomi offered.

"If you like. Naomi, isn't it?"

I decided to follow, and let Wanda talk to Baxter. As we went out, I heard, "I so love teaching police to do their jobs. Anyway, you can tell Hank Jamieson that most of the roof beams are still pretty strong. However, quite a few have signs of water damage, and not just where the roof collapsed."

Outside, Naomi went to look where some trees had branches over the roof. "They are more like to have got in near here. Yes. There, look!"

I glanced and saw the hole, but my attention was caught by the sight of her father trotting out and going over to David, and a stranger, and then all three heading briskly inside.

"Do you think possums could get in there?" Naomi asked me.

"No, but birds might."

Martin brought Lucky-pup over. I took notice of the improvement in the back yard. There was still rusting junk to be removed, but two thirds of the yard was clearer and one of the dad's was using a whipper-snipper to cut down the weeds.

"This little lady has made the acquaintance of the esteemed Rufus," Martin announced. "I think she amuses him."

"I wonder if she can smell out possums," I said aloud. "Wanda found some in the roof and we're trying to find out how they got in."

"Who knows? I will let her smell around. What's happening inside? Did they find something in the roof?"

"Wanda said no, but she may not want to tell us."

"Yeah. Probably, since Kaspersky went in. Come on, let's see what this micro bloodhound can find."

We found one or two possible places that the possums may have got in, and headed back to the laundry.

"...the thing I would like to know, is if Delaney knows about this place being done over," I heard Wanda saying. "That stuff hasn't been disturbed for a long time. Maybe he doesn't know about it, or the stuff was there before he took up with Maude. The only other possibilities are that he has forgotten about it, or thought he could come back and get it whenever he liked."

"We were advised when he got out, but we haven't seen him around here," the man I didn't know was saying. I wondered if he was a policeman.

Wanda saw us hovering and asked, "Find anything?"

"Holes where birds might have got in," Naomi reported. "Not

sure if possums could. We think they might have found a hole where that tree overhangs."

"Or walked along the electricity service wire at the front," I added. "They do that."

"Sounds like your kind of critter," David said, grinning at Wanda. I assumed it was a private joke. She grinned back.

"Later, it might be worth shining a torch through the holes you found and seeing if I can find them from up here. Have they decided between renovation and demolition yet?"

David shook his head. "Right now though, who knows what else we will find."

Kaspersky, picked up a box and brushed some of the dust off. "We will need a locksmith to open this."

Wanda seemed to slide down the ladder. "Let me have a look."

"It's potential evidence."

"Of what? Someone's paranoia? I reckon it predates Delaney's occupation. It might even have been from whoever lived here before Maude."

Kaspersky moved aside and Wanda fiddled with the lock. She had something in her hand. There was a click, and whatever was in her hand went back into a pocket. She opened the box with the policeman looking over her shoulder. I saw her take out a book, and open it.

"1980. This writing is hard to read." She put that aside, and pulled out some papers folded together. "Annie, you are the numbers expert. Can you make anything of this?"

She handed the sheets to me, but I saw her watching me. Did she expect me to pick up on something?

As I looked at the pages, I did seem to sense something. Guilt? Fear? Apprehension? It wasn't really strong.

"It looks like some kind of formula, but I can't say for what. It must have been important, or why hide it."

"Important or dangerous," David suggested. "Or potentially valuable."

I shrugged and handed them back. Wanda was looking through another book, and this one had her fascinated.

"This seems to be a record of something – money transactions."

Wanda passed it to Kaspersky who was soon intent on the contents. "It looks like a record of someone who bets on horse races. One column is for the track, one for the date, one for the race, and the rest for odds and amount and type of bet."

"Is Delaney known for an interest in horse racing?" Wanda asked.

"Not that I am aware of," Kaspersky admitted. "I will check that. But from the dates, I doubt it is relevant."

"What say I go through all this and give you a report of what is there?"

"Okay. See if you can figure out the owner."

"Right. I'll finish in the roof later."

The laundry emptied of most of the bodies, and Naomi shrugged at the bags we had ready. Cleaning suddenly wasn't something I wanted to do. Wanda was putting things carefully back in the box. She surprised me then.

"Here, hold this for a sec. I'll move the ladder."

This time, what I saw was clearer. A man's face, not Delaney, someone younger and reasonable looking. Now, the emotion I had felt before was amplified. The man didn't want the stuff found, someone was after him to get it. He was ashamed about something.

Wanda took the box away, and I snapped back to myself. "Thanks, I will let you get back to cleaning. I'll be in a quiet corner somewhere."

When the last of the trucks had pulled away from the front of the house, Naomi and I took two full bags of confettied paper, mouse shit and disintegrating towels and sheets, out to the skip. The bottles and tins of cleaning stuff were in a box to be taken where they could be safely disposed of.

I saw that the yard was clear, the weeds cut and piled in one corner. Naomi saw where I looked and said, "Dad will probably turn that into a compost heap."

The police dog was having a high time sniffing everywhere. I saw Lucky-pup, her lead tied to a drainpipe, watching the other dog, intently. Martin sidled up from somewhere.

"That mutt thinks she's a bloodhound. She wanted to sniff everything as well."

My dog realised I was there and came over as far as her lead would allow. She wanted to be picked up, so I obliged. Perhaps she wanted a better view, because she was still intent on what the other dog was doing. Then I felt, rather than heard a high pitched whine coming from her. The other dog had stopped and was sniffing at one area, near the big tree. The girls' garden. I recalled Maude saying, "Mickey made it for me."

My mind thought of a horrid possibility and I felt like I wanted to be sick. I passed Lucky-pup to Martin and turned to go inside. I noticed David watching the police dog too, and almost ran into Wanda coming out.

She took me gently by the arm.

"I think they are going to find something," I managed to say.

"So do I," she admitted softly. "But how did you know this time?" She took my hand and opened it from around a tiny figurine that I couldn't recall finding.

"Lucky-pup began to whine. The police dog must have smelt something."

I wanted to cry and to be sick, but then I became aware of Wanda speaking softly, rhythmically, and the nausea went away. "Don't forget that little chant I taught you. It will help. Did you see anything?"

"Not just then."

"Try to remember, that whatever happened here, it was a

long time ago. Today might bring closure to someone.”

“But they might try to blame Maude for it.”

“The police are not out to persecute her.”

I wasn’t so sure, but at least, Wanda was also on Maude’s side. “Will they dig up that garden now?”

“I think they will wait. Did you feel anything from that box I found, or the papers?”

I was glad of the distraction. “Not a lot.” I told her what I could, and she suggested, “Come inside and I will take some notes.”

Episode 9

More Police Attention

Chapter 1
(Annie POV)

After I had given Wanda all the details I could remember from the vision I'd had from the box, I kept myself busy, cleaning, sweeping or removing junk.

"You okay?" Naomi asked me during the afternoon.

"Yeah. I can't help imagining what they will find where the dog was sniffing."

"Me too. At least there was only one spot."

"And we probably won't find out what they find."

"Will probably be in the papers. And give this place an even worse reputation. Dad said that reporters had been bothering him at work. And if they try to talk to us, any of the scouts, we are not to say anything."

"I have no intention of that. Not after meeting that Delaney guy. I'd hate his friends to find me."

"You did a good thing, sticking up for Maude," Naomi told me.

"But I can't do much. I'm only a kid still."

"You said that American woman was on her side."

"Yeah, but she'll have to go back home soon."

"I guess all any of us can do is keep in touch with Maude and let her know she has friends."

Naomi was right, I could do that. I'd just have to find out how.

When Baxter called a halt for the day, I realised that I hadn't seen Wanda since I'd finished detailing my vision. David and the policeman were not around either. I joined the scouts in the kitchen where Baxter was handing out cans of drink. Martin came in with Lucky-pup, and she became as usual, the centre of attention for the younger girls. I doubt they were paying attention when Baxter was thanking everyone for their help. We had finished all the cleaning up we could do. Now they just had to decide between renovating the house or replacement.

As the youngsters were leaving Martin said to Naomi and me, "As soon as this lot go, the police forensic guys will be coming. David said they will put a marquee over the site to protect it and hide it from prying eyes. It is supposed to rain tonight."

"And we will have to wait and see what the police allow the media to print," I said glumly.

"But we will have a better idea that most of the public," Martin pointed out.

"And I hope I am wrong in thinking that they will find Maude's missing girls."

"Is that what you think?" Naomi asked. "It could be just a pet."

"Maude said Mickey made the garden for her. It was the girl's garden," I said.

"Which I reckon means Mickey had to know something," Martin told me. "Or he was trying to make it seem more evidence against Maude."

"Why would he do that?" Naomi asked.

"You don't know him," Martin said. "For which you should be grateful. But whatever his reasons, they probably involved money. He might have been trying to get Maude's inheritance."

"I think we should keep right away from all that and let the police do their job," was Naomi's advice.

"I guess. No, that's the smart thing. Let's hope they put Delaney away for ever. Anyway, I'd better head home. I still have heaps of work to do." I didn't think I could concentrate however.

"Let's stop for ice-cream," Martin suggested. "You can come

too, Naomi."

"Another time. Dad's getting ready to go home."

I was finishing my ice-cream, a Golden Gaytime, when my phone pinged a message. I read it and frowned. Martin raised his brows as if asking what the message was. I passed him my phone.

"What do you make of that?"

"Who's it from?"

"Abbie, I think."

"So, why is she telling you that she may not be at school?"

"Who knows? Most of the time she ignores me, even though I am trying to be friends."

"Ask her how come," Martin suggested.

The answer, when it came, didn't enlighten me. "Mum's packing bags."

I sent, "Holidays?"

"No. Dad is furious about something. I think I know."

I showed that to Martin, and he shrugged.

"I wonder if it is related to the reason he was at police headquarters yesterday?"

"Any idea what Abbie thinks she knows?" Martin asked.

"Nothing that I want to say. I could be imagining things."

I texted, "Can we talk later?"

"She's probably trying for attention," Martin decided. "She can be a bit of a drama queen. We need to keep out of trouble."

"Huh! Did you know that my mum and dad thought this was a nice, quiet neighbourhood? And I seem to be getting known to the police."

When I got home, I tried calling Abbie, but her phone was off. I shrugged and figured I would see her in maths. Or not, if she had in fact gone away with her parents. What did she expect me to do? I had enough on my mind thinking of Maude and what they might find at the scout house.

I went to school in the morning, but felt I should be doing something else. It was stupid, because going to school was what I was meant to be doing.

"Do you get the feeling that school is a waste of time?" I asked Martin when we were almost at the school's back gate.

"Where did that idea come from? Aren't you glad to be going somewhere predictable and safe?"

"School hasn't been predictable since I started here."

"Well, maybe not, but at least now school is better than having to worry about criminals."

Put that way, I had to agree. I needed to stop worrying about things I couldn't affect.

"Did you ever get back to Abbie?" Martin asked?

"No, her phone was off."

"If she turns up, are you going to ask her what it was about?"

"I don't know. She may decide to ignore me."

"I don't know why you bother with her."

By the end of the day, I did too. She acted like I wasn't around, even in maths, although she still sat next to me.

She was lively enough at the breaks with the other Hell's Angels, so I stopped worrying about her.

Karen reckoned she was back to her normal bitchy self, and we had better things to think about. She had been fascinated about my Friday evening and Naomi's account of the working bee on Sunday, and cursed having to play basketball in the afternoon.

"So nothing in the papers?" was her hopeful question.

"It's probably a bit early for that," Naomi suggested. "There might not have been anything newsworthy to find."

As the week progressed, with nothing in the news, I began to relax. That only lasted until Thursday at lunch, and we had a chance to see the newspapers.

"No!" I said after reading the start of the article. I stared at the reproduced photo of Maude's two little girls. The police had dug up the bones of a girl, about three or four years old. It had still been shrouded in a dress that matched that in the photo found at the house. The police hadn't said that it was one of Maude's girls, only that DNA tests would be done on several hairs found caught up in the clothing.

Karen tugged the paper away from me. "They are questioning Mad Maude about it."

"She didn't do it!"

"You might think that now, but she was nuts back then," Karen stated.

"No. She loved those girls. Really looked after them. She only went funny after they were taken away from her."

A new voice commented. "You got a thing for nut cases have you, Jamieson? First Kemple, now that old crackpot."

I pretended I hadn't heard Helen, but Naomi asked, "What do you want? Did Gail tell you to nick off and cause trouble?"

"Nah, she's just having a little private tete-a-tete with dear Abbie. She's been acting downright weird and not pulling her weight."

"You lot making her do your assignments," Naomi challenged, and was rewarded with a scowl.

I took that as a yes, and decided their current bitchiness was because Abbie was too worried about something to do their work as well as her own. And, we had several assignments due in very soon. It would serve them right if they had to knuckle down and do their own work. If they did, they could still finish it in time.

Still, it reminded me of Abbie's cryptic text message. Whatever had caused her to send it, was not something she had shared with her so-called friends.

"Do you know what's bugging her, Jamieson?" Helen demanded, staring at me. "She's been too nice to you lately."

"Nice? You call totally ignoring me as being nice?"

"She told us to lay off you."

"Good for her. Perhaps she isn't a total bitch. But nice? You'd need at least a bit of a smile for that."

The bell went and I was glad of an excuse to hurry away.

For the rest of the afternoon, I couldn't concentrate. Maude's face kept coming to mind. How it had lit up when she talked about her girls. I wondered why the police had kept the find quiet until now, and why they had decided to reveal it. Pressure from the public? It seemed an open secret around the neighbourhood that a body had been found.

On the way home, Martin had a question. "If it's one of Maude's kids, why only one body?"

"Maude called that area the 'Girls' Garden'," I said. "Do you really think...?" I didn't want to say that they still might find another body. "Maude said, Mickey had said, that her Gabbie was alive," I said instead.

"Him? He'd say anything if it made Maude do what he wanted. Perhaps the police said nothing while they looked for a second body."

"The dog was only interested in that one area. And I am pretty sure Wanda checked in the roof, and the police checked under the house after the first find."

"Yeah, and that wasn't a girl," Martin said. "They haven't given out any details beyond it being a male. I wonder if they have identified it yet."

I suddenly wanted to change the subject. "Are you going to try for anything for the sports day?"

Later, I tried to talk to mum about how I felt about Maude, and all the unanswered questions I had about recent events, but she seemed distracted.

"Maude reckoned the girls were put into foster care until she could look after them. They wouldn't have been adopted in that case, would they?"

"They might have been. Since Maude was committed, and it was probably expected that she would not be released. It's only recently that kids in foster care can't be adopted without the parent's okay. Look, Annie, you probably shouldn't involve yourself anymore."

I wasn't listening. "Then why don't the adoptive parents come forward?"

"Darling, back then, the birth parents and the adoptive parents never learnt anything about each other. The details were sealed."

I almost blurted out what Abbie had said, but her case was different. Carson had said he was her father. Then a little voice in my head said, *"Carson had a birth certificate for Gabrielle Hartley."* Another voice said, *"Anyone could order a birth certificate,"* countered by, *"Why would they without a reason?"*

I left mum alone, and went back to my room. Surely, if Maude had sex with him, she would remember? Wanda had determined that her memory was good. She didn't recognise the name, only said he looked familiar. Would Carson have changed a lot in a dozen years?

Say he had, and Abbie's fears about him being a conman were justified? Was that the answer? Was he intending to pass Abbie off as Maude's daughter, and control a lot of money through her?

I ought to write a novel, I decided. I had too much imagination and no proof. Not even to decide if Maude did or did not kill her kids.

The subject kept intruding on my concentration, and finally caused me to open my email program with the intention of sending Wanda an email. Her opinion might be different to mine, or more sympathetic than my mother's. Before that though, I answered some emails from my friends of last year. Only then did I open a new email and try to form a coherent message from the 'it's not fair' chaos in my mind. Finally I settled on, "Have you heard about the other body they found? Do they really think that Maude did it?"

I hoped for a reply before I went to bed, but Wanda and her husband might be on the plane back home for all I knew.

I didn't expect to have my message answered in person, but half way to school, a shadow slipped out of cover and greeted us.

"Morning!"

I spun around. "Oh! You startled me. Why are you here?"

"I wondered if there was any more to your query."

"I thought you might have gone back home."

"Got caught up with some genealogical research. My unlamented grandfather had cousins out here."

"Oh. Then you haven't seen Maude?"

Wanda shook her head. "Like I said, we are foreign consultants. In theory, we can't push into local investigations."

"The paper said they were questioning her. They think one of her kids is buried in the garden."

Martin had to correct me. "They didn't go that far."

"But they implied it!"

"Let's stay calm and keep walking. You don't want to be late." She was right.

"Of course they are talking to Maude," Wanda went on. "She used to live there. They've tried questioning Mickey, but he's not saying anything."

"But what if they think she killed the little girl."

"You don't think it was one of hers?" Wanda was looking

right into me.

"They sound pretty sure it is. The clothes and all are the ones the kids had on in the birthday picture."

"They are running DNA tests. That should settle the matter. And even if they think Maude guilty, they will have to prove it and she has an excellent lawyer."

"They can't charge her for that – I mean, she's done time."

"Not for that," Martin corrected me again. "That was for kidnapping."

"That is a pertinent point," Wanda admitted. "But she was declared unfit for trial back then, and even though she is better now –"

"You mean she'll be declared as being unfit then," I asked hopefully.

"If I were her lawyer, that's what I would be saying – if worst comes to worst."

"What do you think happened?" I asked.

"It was a long time ago. Memories blur."

"That's not an answer."

"No, it isn't. I am keeping an open mind."

"How come you haven't gone home yet?" I asked. "You mentioned family history."

"Them? Well, I just wanted to find out if there are any relatives that I haven't learnt about. I think most of them are known."

"Like known to the police?" Martin asked.

"Hmmm."

"Do you think they were involved with that other business in the park?" Martin asked.

"This better go no further, but it is the sort of business they would go in for and they do have multitudinous overseas connections. David has been searching on-line. Which reminds me, any chance you can introduce me to Abbie Carson? She goes to your school doesn't she?"

"Yes, but she hasn't been talking to me. And their new housekeeper picks her up and drops her off. Why?"

"What happened to the old housekeeper?"

"Got fired. She had to go off to tend a relative, and rang their house before Abbie's dad rang to say he and her mum would be away a while."

"So...she was on her own?"

I glanced at Martin then. I hadn't intended to say so much. "Yes. I think for about two weeks."

Martin whistled. "Then she has more guts than I thought."

"Have you seen her at the milkbar?" I asked Martin.

"Not anymore," Martin confirmed. "But she is meant to be doing community service."

"Okay, that might be something."

Before I could censor it, I blurted, "Is this about her father being married twice?"

Wanda gave that scrutinising look again. "Lots of people have been married more than once. My dad has been married three times."

"No, I mean, married to two women at once."

"Carson?" Martin scoffed. "Mr holier than thou?"

I had never met Abbie's father, but I had heard Martin call him that before.

"Then I doubt he'd admit it to anyone in his family," Wanda predicted. "What made you ask? One of your flashes?"

I nodded cautiously. Not comfortable with the spot I had put myself in. Not even Abbie knew that I knew some things. This time I was remembering something I had seen and forgotten. I needed to check my journal, and add some things to it as well.

"What else have you picked up from her?"

"Stuff. But I might be wrong."

"So far, you have been on the mark."

"You won't say who told you?"

"On that, you have my word. I am quite sure that none of the local police will accept 'I got it from a psychic', so I am not even going to imply it. What I can do is assume it is correct and have it as a starting point to check stuff online."

"I don't really feel like saying anything. Abbie's dad is already angry with her as it is."

"Fair enough."

Wanda didn't push for me to tell, and I was grateful for that. "Let me know if you change your mind. Just remember, I am not a member of the local police. I have no requirement to pass on what I know, unless it relates to the case I came here for."

"What did you want to talk to Abbie about? Does it have anything to do with Maude?" That was also on my mind.

"I don't think so."

Wanda seemed to be waiting for me to speak again, but I didn't want to say any more. Not yet, anyway.

"Then why are you interested in Carson?" Martin asked.

"Just helping an old retired police friend. I need something to do with myself while David is checking people out."

"Why aren't you helping him?" Martin persisted.

"Well, the thing is, I don't want those people to know I am around."

"What do you want to know about Carson?"

"Carson asked his police friend to help him with a personal problem. He thinks someone is trying to blackmail him. My friend, the retired policeman, was asked to look into it."

I couldn't help wondering if that was why Abbie's dad was in a foul mood, but then, a memory of another of my flashes surfaced. The one about the brochure and Abbie's textiles teacher. Again, I wondered if I should mention it, but Abbie had asked me not to.

My attention went back to Wanda when she said, "I'd better let you both get a hurry on. I will find some other way to talk to your friend."

Martin waited until Wanda had headed back the way we had come before asking, "Do you know other things about Abbie?"

"Nothing I would want to swear to," I told him.

Martin accepted that and changed the subject to the school sports day, coming up in a fortnight. "You going to try out for anything?"

"Maybe running. At my last school, competing was voluntary."

"I thought you might be into high jump, or discus, since you like the maths and physics stuff."

"You don't do those with your head. I did try long jump but I always fell back on my butt. What about you?"

"Oh, I like shotput. It fits my delinquent image. Some people think I go round chucking rocks at windows."

I had to laugh. "Do they really? Or are you just trying to see how dumb people can be?"

The answer to that was a chuckle.

We reached the school gate and I saw a couple of people inside, leaning against the high wire fence. They were too old to be students. The young bloke looked like a bikie, the girl had on a purple-dyed leather vest and matching leggings. Her hair was hidden under a beanie. I nudged Martin when I sensed the man staring at me. The regard made me uneasy.

Martin said in a whisper for me to keep going, and in my side vision, I saw him going over towards them. I heard him say, "I don't know why you are here, and I don't want to, but you should be warned that the police patrol along here quite often at this time of day."

"Thanks, mate, but it's no problem. Just want a quick word with our little sister."

"Step-sister," the woman corrected. "Your girlfriend is a lot like her."

"Who is she?" I heard Martin ask. I wasn't going away that fast.

"Abbie," the woman said. "Bit of a spoilt princess she is."

"Abbie Carson?"

"Yeah. You know her?" the bloke asked.

"She's in some of my classes," Martin admitted. I decided to move back to hear more. "I could take her a message."

"Don't want stuff in writing. Just need to talk to her. Can you get her to come here later?"

I got there and said, "We're only allowed back here when arriving or leaving."

"After school then," the man insisted. "I've seen her come this way a few times."

That admission gave me shivers. *Who were these two?*

"Not often," Martin told him. "She used to catch the bus from out the front."

"Now she gets delivered and picked up by the housekeeper," I said.

The man ran fingers back through his hair. "Okay, can you give her my number?"

"Probably," I said. If Abbie gave me a chance to speak to her. "Got a pen? And paper?"

"What's your name?" I asked, as I dropped my pack and went to a side pocket. I kept a notepad there, with a pen. "Her father is being a right jerk at the moment. Doesn't want her talking to people he doesn't like."

When I passed the items over, I deliberately brushed the guy's hand. He was looking down, so wouldn't have seen my reaction to the startlingly vivid flash I had of the girl with Abbie. She had spiked purple hair then.

The man scribbled the number. "I'm Robbo. She knows us."

I said, casually. "I didn't know she had siblings."

"We only found out recently. She's a nice kid, and we'd like to keep in touch. We're heading away, soon."

Something in the woman's tone didn't sit right with the sentiment she admitted.

"We tried to re-connect with our father, but he's set the police on us for stalking him."

That had a ring of truth to it.

"That sounds like something that bastard would do," Martin admitted. "He and I had words last year. He didn't think I was a suitable friend for his daughter."

"You couldn't have stood up very well next to his opinion of himself," Robbo said.

Martin laughed. "No. I wasn't rich. Abbie hangs out with the supposedly rich clique. He probably told her to."

"And now he's mad at her because the boyfriends of her 'friends' got her into trouble," I added.

The look that came onto the man's face was malicious. I shivered again. He said, "Carson is an enormous hypocrite. Anyway, thanks for seeing Abbie gets that."

"I can't guarantee that she'll call you," I decided to say.

Just then the first bell rang. I tugged Martin's arm, to get him to hurry. We didn't want to be late for homeroom.

After leaving Martin and Annie, Wanda returned to the hired car and asked the driver to take her back to the home of ex-CI Kelso. The driver, another retired policeman, followed her inside. David looked up from his laptop computer and grinned.

"How did your chat go?" Kelso asked.

"Annie doesn't think Maude would have hurt her girls," Wanda summarised. "Are the DNA results back yet?"

"No. Did you find a way to talk to Carson's daughter?"

"I have ruled out going to Carson's place. Sounds like he has her incommunicado out of school hours. Has the new housekeeper dropping her off and picking her up."

"Probably wants to keep her out of trouble," Kelso proposed.

"My father tried that and it didn't work," Wanda told him. "And I don't think that questioning her at school would be any better. We'd have to have a teacher present and word that she was being questioned would get around."

"What does that leave? After school activities?"

"Like I said, sounds like she is confined to the house after school. However, Annie mentioned that she had to do community service. I thought you might be able to get me working where she is."

Kelso twisted to talk to his driver. "See what you can find out, will you, Fred." He turned back and told her, "Seems that your two young friends met some people when they got to school."

David explained, "I had a call from some officious type asking if I had just been near the school."

"As if you'd admit it if you were and not meant to be," Wanda stated the obvious.

"I told him that I was in a meeting with Atlas Task Force Officers, and did he need me to have them confirm it."

Wanda chuckled. "Do you know who the people were?"

"No, but Kelly is heading to the school to get a look at the schools CCTV. He will go back again to catch Annie and Martin before they leave. The Acting Head, the one I talked to, is sure they were not telling him everything."

"It's likely," Wanda considered. "I think Annie has picked up some things that she is still not sure about telling anyone. Even me."

"Do you think those two loiterers wanted to talk to Abbie Carson?" Kelso said sharply.

"I have no idea."

"Gill, the acting head, told Kelly all that the kids had told him. The kids claimed not to know who the two strangers were or what they wanted. He thought the male had written something and given it to Annie. She admitted lending him a notepad and pen, but the last entry had been David's number."

"What made you ask about Abbie?"

Kelso frowned. "As I told you, Carson claims he was being set up – probably for blackmail. He didn't give Des anything to work on. He mentioned a break in at his house a week or so back, but hadn't reported it to the police because nothing had been taken. Des told him there was nothing he could do. However, I offered to help out, mainly because you had said Maude Delaney and her lawyer thought they recognised him."

"Have you learnt anything?" Wanda asked.

Again, David spoke up. "I have managed to access the security cams from several properties in Carson's street. There has been a car lurking that isn't registered to anyone in the street. It might just be a visitor. The car's registered to a hire company, but the names they gave us are probably false. I am just working back to see if I spot anything. Kelly has permission to copy the footage from the school this morning. Gill thinks the people are related to those selling drugs, and that is what Martin isn't saying."

"No!" Wanda disagreed instantly.

"Oh, I agree," David grinned. "I don't think Gill likes Martin, and wants him caught out. So, he is happy to help Kelly."

"Actually, Annie did say something about the Carson household. The current housekeeper hasn't worked there very long. The previous one was fired, probably unjustly. Seems, Carson left a message at the house, at the last minute, saying he and his wife would be away. But that was after she had called him about a family emergency. Annie thinks Abbie was on her own for two weeks."

Kelso straightened. "When was this?"

"I didn't ask for dates, but I assume it was just before she got herself in trouble. Fred might be able to find out when she was in court."

"Maybe we should talk to the previous housekeeper," Kelso mused. "See if she had any inking of threats against Carson. I will see about finding her and get the local boys to talk to her."

"So, you implied Carson didn't mention any particular misdemeanour he could be blackmailed for?"

"No."

"One thing. Annie asked me if my questions related to Carson being married to two women at the same time."

Kelso stood, "I think we should look closer at Jeremy Carson. He might be peripheral to all this business with Maude Delaney, but I think he isn't as innocent as he proclaims. I will speak to Des. What will you do now?"

"Go and see if Fred has found where Abbie will be doing hard labour."

Kelly arrived late morning and downloaded a copy of the schools CCTV file onto the computer David was using. All of them looked at the replay and at a certain point, David stopped it and enlarged the faces of the two loiterers.

"Get a screen shot of them," Kelso directed. "I will have Des request a search through the mug files."

He then sent Kelly to find out about Carson's former housekeeper, and to arrange for someone to question her.

Kelso's request to his former protégé resulted in that officer coming to visit them.

"What are you stirring up, old man?" Des Kingley greeted. "A retired cop and two foreign investigators are not meant to stir up trouble. I can disable your access to active cases."

"I am only trying to find out who has it in for Carson," Kelso protested. "However, there was that woman recently who thought he was in that time share scam a few years ago. The leader of that was never caught."

"You think that might be Carson? I'd say it was unlikely - I've known him for years."

"He could have a hundred secrets that you don't know, and be using friendship with you as a character reference."

Wanda decided to comment, "The best con artists don't look like con artists."

The senior policeman, gave her a considering stare. "How much longer will you two be staying?"

"David and I have permission to keep an eye on things here for a bit. Our superiors aren't convinced that the people we are after have left Australia. And, in that role, any chance of getting permission to speak to Mickey Delaney?"

"What about?"

"Who hired him, where he met that person and what his orders were."

"We tried that and he won't talk," Kingly told her. "I don't think he would talk to you."

"Maybe I should ask him about things he did before he went to prison."

"No, Mrs Davis. That is still an active investigation."

An unfazed Wanda, merely grinned. "The offer stands."

"I will allow you to look into Carson. If you find anything bring it to the old man. I don't expect you to have any success."

"And if I do?"

"OK. See if you can come up with anything and if I see a basis for further investigation, then I will get him in to talk to him," Des agreed.

There was no time for me to talk to Martin since we had to race to get to our homeroom, however, before we reached there, Mr Gill intercepted us. We couldn't exactly ignore him.

"Who were you both talking to at the back gate?"

While I was held speechless by the unexpected question, Martin said, "They said they were waiting to talk to their sister. I told them we weren't allowed back there during school hours. I was going to mention them to Mrs Sutton when we got to class."

"One of them passed something to you, Miss Jamieson," Gill accused. I wondered who had been spying on us.

"Yes. Handing it back. I suggested they could write a message for us to deliver. I offered pen and my notepad," I admitted. "I thought I might have found out who they wanted to talk to, but they didn't want anything in writing."

"Rather than try to play detective, you should have stayed clear of them," Gill lectured.

"You won't get me disagreeing," I told him immediately. My conscience was prickling me, but I wasn't sure I wanted to tell him everything.

"I will have a look at your notepad."

I didn't dare glance at Martin, just dropped my backpack, found the notepad and handed it over. Gill opened it and glanced through the pages with writing on. I'd made miscellaneous notes on some and had several phone numbers there already. One of them was Robbo's.

Gill showed me the last page with writing on. "Whose number is this?"

"Can I have a better look? I've met a number of people recently." I was trying to delay answering, and I knew it. *What should I tell him?*

Martin gave me an out. "That guy didn't actually write anything, did he?"

"He looked like he was considering it," I said, as I studied the number. "I know! That's David's number. Did he give you a card, Martin?"

"Yes. Wait a sec." Martin pulled out his wallet and had a look. "Got it. What's the number?"

I read it out. "Yup. That's it."

Martin handed the card to Gill so he could check for himself. The card didn't say what David was. When Gill took out his mobile phone to ring the number, Martin looked my way so Gill couldn't see the faint grin on his face.

I watched Gill's face. He introduced himself and asked if David had been near the school just now. While he listened for the reply, I saw the faintest flush suffuse Gill's face. He spoke stiffly, saying, "No Sir, that won't be necessary."

After replacing his phone in his pocket, he handed the notepad back to me and told us to hurry to class.

"Why didn't you tell him?" Martin asked as we crouched at our lockers to get what we needed for class.

"Thought I was going to have to," I admitted. "But then I remembered that the guy had opened it at the back, and wrote on that page."

Martin chuckled. "When will you give it to Abbie?"

"When I can talk to her alone. I think that's fair. She doesn't need more grief from her father, and I reckon those two we saw are the reason he's been acting like a jerk."

"What if Gill calls the police?"

"So what? We just tell it as it was."

"And give them the phone number?"

"Maybe," I hedged. "I wasn't comfortable around those two, but I don't think they are out to harm Abbie."

"Well, I hope you are right. I got the impression those two have been living hard."

"Committing crimes?" I was sure of at least one crime.

"Probably. Might have been in jail, too."

"Are you saying I should tell Gill?"

"Hell no! Not him. I was thinking Wanda, or David."

"I'll call her later. After I give the number to Abbie."

I couldn't talk to Abbie in class and during the breaks she was well guarded by her friends. My last idea was to catch her on the way to the housekeeper's car. The Hells Angels had usually hurried to the bus by then.

It didn't happen. My phone pinged its message tone. Martin had sent, "Gill's looking for you." There was only one thing that could be about.

I saw Abbie, and ran over to her. "Abbie!" She didn't even acknowledge that she had heard me. Just kept walking straight ahead. *What the hell was bugging her?*

I turned away, not particularly wanting to see Gill, but had the choice taken from me. Ms Sutton, who was on front gate duty, gave me the same message. *Oh well, I'd better see what he wants.*

I could do without the pontifical advice about hanging around with Martin and how I might end up. But Martin winked at me and I relaxed.

"Did you just want us here to say that, Sir?" I asked.

He glared at me. "No, Miss Jamieson. Someone is coming here to talk to you both."

The phone on Gill's desk rang. He answered it, listened, thanked someone and told us, "He has arrived. Stay here."

Martin and I collapsed into chairs. I heard him mutter his impression of Gill.

I recognised the voice of the person returning with Gill. He might be trying to make us feel guilty, but he wasn't going to convince Detective Kelly that we'd been doing something criminal.

His casual greeting didn't sit well with Gill, who went to sit behind his desk.

"What did you need us for, Sir?" Martin asked, showing Gill he wasn't worried about this meeting.

"I understand you were talking to some trespassers this morning."

"Yes."

"Tell me about them."

I let Martin do the talking, going over the conversation, giving his opinions, and describing them.

"Are they the people who you saw hanging around at the start of term?" Kelly asked.

"No, I am sure they aren't," Martin told him.

"Can you think of anything else?" Kelly asked, including me in his gaze.

My conscience pricked me. "I think the woman called the guy Robbo."

Kelly made a note of that.

"Can I ask what this is about?"

"We are still working to find all the people involved in that business at the start of term," Kelly said. "Keep up the good work, and let your teachers know if you see anyone else acting odd."

"Can we head off now?" Martin asked.

"Yes. I have what I needed," Kelly confirmed. "Want a ride home?"

"No thanks. I have to keep fit for sports day next week," I claimed. I don't think Gill was happy about the casual offer.

I was glad to leave his office.

Martin gestured to me to get out of sight. Bemused, I did as he suggested. Kelly was on his phone as he walked slowly towards the front of the school. The parent parade was thinning out. Once Martin had figured out which car Kelly was aiming for, he gestured for me to start walking. He wanted to get there ahead of the detective.

"Well, did you think of something else?" Kelly drawled. "Or have questions you didn't want to shock Gill by asking."

"Yeah, like that," Martin agreed. "We didn't tell Gill everything this morning. Those two we spoke to wanted to talk to Abbie Carson. Said she was their step-sister."

My conscience prickled me again. "I did get Robbo's phone number. Gill didn't see it, because he didn't look at the last page." I took the pad from my pocket. "I wanted to give it to Abbie first, but she wouldn't listen to me."

Kelly took the book and copied the number. "Did it occur to you to question what they were intending besides talk?"

"Yes, but ... I didn't feel they were planning to hurt Abbie."

"There's such a thing as being too trusting," Kelly remarked. "Perhaps you can explain why you felt like that to your friend Wanda?"

"Okay."

"How did Abbie Carson seem today?" Kelly asked.

"She didn't want to talk to me."

"Stiffer necked than normal," Martin added his opinion.

"Do you think she was worried about something?"

I considered that. "Yeah, that might have been her problem. Why ask?"

Kelly just shook his head.

Wanda's phone rang, and she quickly drew it from her pocket. Very few people had the number. She checked the display. "Hello Annie," she answered. "What's up?"

"Can we talk to you?"

"Sure. When and where?"

"How about the park?"

"Will Martin be with you?"

"Yes."

"Why not at his place? Will be more private."

"Um," Annie paused and Wanda could hear her talking in the background. "That's okay. I won't be able to stay long. I have to be home by four-thirty."

"I can be there in fifteen minutes." Wanda ended the call.

David's brows were raised in enquiry as she made a call of her own.

"Kelly, do you happen to know why Annie wants to talk to me?"

She heard, "I suggested it. Like an unofficial chat."

"Okay. Like that. You've just spoken to them?"

"Yes."

"Well. I've got myself assigned to the park detail tomorrow. Abbie Carson is meant to be there. I hope to get her talking."

"Be careful. Seems her father is being very protective."

"I can handle the likes of him."

Kelly chuckled and rang off. Wanda gave David a quick summary. "Want to come?"

"You likely to need me?" he teased, and was not surprised when she blew a raspberry at him.

Fred was perfectly happy to drive her to the corner of Martin's street. He confided that things were livelier since she and David had arrived. He also agreed to wait nearby. She was just getting out of the car when she caught sight of Annie, trying to be unobtrusive near a house just along the main road.

"Just wait a bit here, Fred. I want to talk to that girl up there. If I head up the side street without her, keep an eye on her."

Wanda closed the car door quietly, and casually strolled across the end of Martin's street and approached Annie.

"Hi," she said quietly. Annie still jumped.

"Oh. Sorry. Martin was getting annoyed by his cousins, and I didn't want to go to his place if they were there."

"His cousins. He did mention them. Weren't they involved in that business at your school at the start of term?"

"Yes, they were suspended. I think they can start back again on Monday."

"I might just wander up and see what's what. If anyone bothers you here, I have asked my driver to keep an eye on you. His name is Fred, and he's in the blue car just back there. He's an ex-policeman, and really sweet."

"Thank you."

Wanda heard the mock fight from two houses away. She was impressed by Martin's self-control. It sounded like the two older boys were trying to get him angry. They sounded at least a little bit drunk.

"Gentlemen? Is there a problem here?"

She spoke loud enough to be heard and shared her regard equally between the three, not showing that she already knew Martin. He was the first to reply.

"Not if these two leave as I asked."

"We just came to see how our cuz was doing," Tom claimed.

"Cousins? I see. Well then maybe I need to speak to both of you as well."

"Huh? Us? We haven't done anything," Gerry said, suddenly wary.

"How about public drunkenness?" Wanda suggested. Both boys backed away.

"What's the bespoleznyy otrod'ye trying to accuse us of?" Tom asked defiantly.

"Is there something that he should?" Wanda asked, with a questioning widening of her eyes. "I'd be happy to provide witness for him as a member of the local neighbourhood watch."

That seemed to be enough for the twins. One leant down to retrieve a sixpack of beer, and both backed away and took off further up the street.

"You can let Annie know it's safe to come up," Wanda suggested. She took her own phone and tapped in a number. "Fred? Can I get you to see where a couple of young louts go?" She waited for agreement and described Martin's cousins. "Thanks."

Martin had finished his call. "I like your style! But those two are pretty harmless. I think their step-father would kill them if they got in real trouble."

"Well, from what you told me, they are on the fringe of trouble now. Their step-father isn't really keeping them in line."

"They are meant to keep away from me," Martin admitted. "But they think since I have my place to myself now, it's a good place to hide out and get drunk."

"What's with this bespoleznyy otrod'ye business?"

Martin shrugged. "They've been coming out with that recently. I don't know what it means, and they think it funny that I don't."

"It means something like 'useless brat' in Russian. Is their step-father Russian?"

"I don't think so."

"Hmm. Anyway, here's Annie. You should ask them if their step-father calls them that."

"I might at that," Martin grinned.

"Are they gone?" Annie asked as Fred's car drove past.

Martin laughed. "With tail between legs. Come in."

Martin did a quick tidy of the front room after dumping his school bag. Once they had all settled in chairs, Wanda got to the point.

"Kelly suggested you talk to me, right? I already know you met some people after you got to school. Tell me about them."

What they'd said, agreed with what she'd heard from Kelly. "So what was it that you didn't want to tell him?"

Annie was looking uncomfortable, she was twisting the fabric of her skirt, and also broadcasting thoughts of all the things she was trying to find the words for.

"Let me guess," Wanda said quietly. "While you were around Abbie, you picked certain things up."

Annie nodded, then blurted, "Those two, this morning? I saw them around Abbie. I think they were inside her place. And today, when I took my notebook back, I touched the guy. I saw that same meeting, I think, but from his point of view. Abbie and that woman this morning."

"Interesting," Wanda murmured. "Carson told a policeman friend about a break in, a week or so ago."

"Yes!" Annie agreed. "It was while Abbie's parents were away, and she was alone at home. I think she told her folks about it, but not until a week later. I don't think she mentioned those two. They said they were her step-sibs."

"How old do you think they were?" Wanda asked. Annie shrugged, but Martin guessed, "About your age?"

"Late twenties," Wanda admitted. "We took an image from the school's CCTV. The faces are being run through the books to see if we get a match."

"So that must have been how Gill saw what we were doing," Annie said, enlightened.

"Probably," Wanda agreed. "Now, was there any other vision

you've had about Abbie that might help?"

She listened, but nothing seemed useful until Annie said, "I saw her father getting angry, and telling her something. I didn't get sound, but whatever it was, I think that's what made her run off."

"And you have no idea about it?" Wanda prompted. "Remember, this conversation is so far off the record so as not to exist."

"Well, I know Abbie had her birth certificate at school. Her friends are on about getting their learners and they need that for it. But...I don't know how it's connected to what her father was ranting about. I just feel it is."

Somehow she still couldn't bring herself to mention the name on the certificate. She managed, "I somehow don't think that her mother is her real mother."

It was the closest she could come. It didn't mean that Abbie was really Gabrielle Hartley, only that her father night be planning something illegal. He hadn't done anything yet. Instead, she mentioned about the teacher at school.

"Yes, I heard a report from someone about that," Wanda admitted. "So that's it?"

Annie nodded. "What will you do about what I said?"

"Try and get Abbie to tell me herself. I'll be seeing her tomorrow."

Episode 10

Daddy's Girl
(Abbie's POV)

Chapter 1

Abbie was glad to be rid of Gail and the others. Their petty disgruntlement at her lack of funds was beyond unpleasant. They thought she was holding back on them, and she was, but only so that she'd have money in the bank for emergencies. She had told them that her dad wasn't going to give her any allowance until she had finished her community service. He had told her he wasn't going to reward her for being a stupid fool and breaking the law.

No need for her to tell them that her mother was slipping her a few dollars now and then.

The only reason why she had hung around them all day was so little Miss Helpful would keep away from her.

Annie was okay, really. Nice but she was freaky, knowing things from just touching stuff. She didn't dare let her get too close.

Her father, well he was like an explosion waiting to happen. Her mother had said they might have to leave at a moment's notice. The bags were still packed, just in case. Neither of her parents had told her what the trouble was, but it hadn't come to a head, until today.

Her mother had texted, "The police came around to ask your father questions." She hadn't said about what. Abbie's mind came up with a number of possibilities. They might have found out she'd been abandoned at home for two weeks. Or her teacher might have gone to them with the insane idea that he'd scammed her. Or had Robbo and Thea alleged something. That might be it. That might have been why he had stormed off the other day to see his police friend. Those two very definitely hated her father, but were they really related to him?

They were still about. She'd had a glimpse of them in a car as Mrs Buttrose drove her to school. They had said they'd be in touch, but since then, her father had changed her phone number. She wasn't even sure she wanted to talk to them. They made her uncomfortable. What would they do if he refused to talk to them, or put the police on them? He said he had to have a spotless reputation or he'd lose his job. And she herself would be shunned by Gail and the others. Even more than they were doing now.

"Abbie!"

Abbie didn't turn. She didn't want to talk to Miss Goody Two Shoes. She just wanted to get home and find out the worst.

"Mum?" Abbie called as soon as she was in the front door. She followed the sound of her Mother's voice to her father's office.

"....just do it! Jeremy needs the funds available as soon as possible."

Victoria Carson saw her daughter in the doorway and ended the conversation. "Let me know when the transfer has been done."

"Mum? What's wrong? Why did the police have questions for Daddy?"

"Probably because someone is trying to get him in trouble," Victoria said at once.

For a moment, Abbie considered mentioning Robbo and Thea, but the compulsion died immediately.

"Jeremy wants us to go away for a bit. Just until he sorts out the problem. So go and get any last minute things you want to take. We will be leaving tonight."

"I can't! Mum, I've got that community service stuff to do tomorrow. It will be every week until I've done the hours. And what about school?"

"Your Dad will sort things out," Victoria told her.

Abbie turned and ran to her room. Her father was in trouble. If he was sending them away, it must mean he didn't trust her. She grabbed her phone, the IPad she'd just got back off Gail, her kindle, plus her few pieces of really valuable jewellery and her journal. She tried to think of anything else she wouldn't want to lose if she didn't come back. There was still most of her clothes, all her stuffed animals, her CD collection – she'd take her favourites of those – and her magazines.

The door slammed downstairs. Her father's voice reached her ears but she couldn't make out what he was saying. Abbie ventured from her room, but kept out of sight at the top of the stairs.

"Des doesn't think there is any substance to the allegations, but he had to ask me questions. I've told him I can provide records back to 2000, but he didn't think that necessary. However, I am not convinced that someone isn't out to get at me. So I need you and Abbie out of the way. Go up north, to your cousin's place."

Victoria reminded her husband of what Abbie had said.

"Yes. I can't do anything about that. It should still be safe enough tomorrow, then we will see. The little chit might be safer if she were locked up, but I would rather avoid that publicity."

Abbie retreated to her room and went to the window. Her room looked out onto the back yard, and she moved her curtains wondering if she could get out that way. Movement in the yard caught her attention. Thea was down there, near one of the big trees. In black clothes, she was harder to see. Thea waved, then held something light coloured up, and then put it down under the tree. Finally, she pointed up at the window – at her – then towards the tree.

Abbie stepped back, hearing someone in the passage. Was Thea leaving something there for her? When the footsteps went past, she returned to the window, gave Thea a thumbs up, and watched her disappear behind the tree. What could it be? Abbie wasn't sure she wanted to go and get it, and certainly not right away.

More movement in the passage caused her to pull out her folder and English text, and sit at her desk. She could look like she was doing homework, while she thought about things. Better yet, she would pretend to be listening to music too.

Once again, she wondered if she should mention that woman. Somehow, she couldn't really imagine being related to them. Yet they had known how obsessive he was. And then there was that freaky thing Annie had said about her father. It fit with what her so-called sibs had claimed.

What if her father dumped her and her mother? What would they do? Was making them go away the first step to him going away? Changing his name again? If she told her father about Robbo and Thea, would that make him worse?

By the time she was called down for tea, her stomach was too tense for her to want to eat. She would have to bluff, pretend she didn't know anything, not even the little her mother had told her.

They ate in silence for a while before Carson asked her, "How would you like to take some time off school?"

"What's that?" She looked up in surprise. Her mother had said about it, but he had always insisted she never missed school.

"My grandmother is very sick," Victoria explained. "She has

never met you, and I think you would brighten her day."

Abbie dutifully reminded her father about her community service obligation. Her mind was telling her that whatever he said, he wouldn't be telling her the truth.

"Well, yes, I expect you will need to go tomorrow. But I am sure I can swing something with my friend Des Kingley."

"And I'd not like to get behind with my work."

"I will fix that with the school." He waved that aside.

"Well, okay I guess." Abbie couldn't think what else to say. "I don't think I can eat any more. Can I be excused? I want to get an assignment finished so I can email it to Mrs Sutton tonight."

Jeremy Carson smiled. Abbie kept her glee hidden inside. He had brought her dutiful act — more fool him. Maybe she'd have more freedom away from home? No, he'd make sure she didn't. He wanted some mythical inheritance.

Wanda was already digging over a garden bed when Abbie was led over and told what to do. She was given a shovel and left to it. Her first efforts were half hearted. She had absolutely no experience with gardening. She didn't look at her fellow worker, so Wanda maintained her own expression of not wanting to be there. After all, she didn't want to seem too friendly and inquisitive.

"Are you going to use that thing or just let it hold you up?" Wanda growled after a quarter hour had passed. "When they come back later and see you aren't working, they'll get right narky."

"I don't know what to do," Abbie said.

Deciding not to point out that the instructions had been clear enough, Wanda explained. "We need to dig out the weeds and dead stuff, so they can put in new flowers. And we need to remove or break up the roots so the weeds don't grow again. Also, breaking up the topsoil and turning it over helps aerate the soil."

"Oh." Abbie did make more of an effort, but it was obvious she had never done such physical stuff.

Wanda was used to digging, and this was much easier than the heavy digging that was needed on her and David's hobby farm in California.

"Look, kid. Why don't I dig, and you pick up the weeds, and shake the dirt off them?"

"Okay," Abbie said with relief.

"Didn't they give you gloves?"

"Ah, no."

"Here! Use these," Wanda offered. "I'd say you need them more than me."

Once again, Wanda fell silent. She hoped Abbie would

initiate the next conversation, but the girl would have to decide that the tough character she had been paired with, was no threat to her.

Finally, "How come you are doing this?" Abbie asked in a quiet voice. "What did you do?"

"Me? Nothing. The cops had it in for me."

"No, really," Abbie asked.

"Oh, alright. I had a blow off with my boyfriend and went off in his car."

"Was that all?"

"Geeze, you're persistent! No. I was a bit pissed and kinda forgot you drive on a different side of the road here. I had to swerve to avoid a car. No one was hurt."

"Had you been drinking?"

"Not enough to ring their bell!" Wanda went on with her made up story. "My boyfriend told them he let me use his car, so I wasn't charged with pinching it."

"But?"

"They got kinda narked when I skittled a few full garbage wheelie bins."

The image made Abbie laugh, and finally relax. "What about you, kid?"

"I'm Abbie. I just got caught with my boyfriend, when I was meant to stay away from him."

"Spoil sports," Wanda muttered.

"No, I should have stayed away. Adam was okay, but his brother..."

"Was a bastard? Did he get anywhere?"

"No. Not really. The police turned up."

"Well, you'll be wiser now, I expect."

"My dad has been poisonous ever since."

"Worried about his reputation, is he?"

"I don't think it's only that." Abbie said, then went silent.

Wanda let her be. She still had time enough to encourage her to speak. She would work certain trigger words into her conversation. Ideas got from talking to Annie the previous day.

When the silence had gone on for half an hour, Wanda said, "You got any brothers or sisters, kid?"

"No." Abbie tensed, but saw the woman wasn't even looking at her. "Do you?"

"Yeah. Lost count how many. Had three when I walked out on my old man. Ran into my sister a while back. Had four more by then. Might even have more by now. I don't think my old man even misses me."

"Mine wants to keep me locked up."

"Mine tried that. Even hired a security guard."

"What did you do?"

"Left anyway."

"I tried that. That's how I ended up here."

One of the full time gardeners approached with a wheel barrow to collect the piled weeds. He also grabbed two bottles of water from a back pack for them. He grunted, "You two are working real well."

Abbie smiled, not expecting the complement. "Do we get a break?"

"Take ten minutes if you like. Lunch is at 12.30." He quickly transferred the weeds and went off.

Abbie collapsed onto the ground with a grateful sigh. "I haven't been allowed out by myself for over a month."

"You sure he hasn't got anyone watching you?" Wanda had noticed a man sitting on a bench, within eye shot. She had recognised him and already alerted David using a mike hidden under her collar.

"Why?" Abbie asked, sitting up suddenly and looking around.

"Take it easy," Wanda cautioned. "Guy on the seat."

"You think he's watching us?" Abbie kept her voice low.

"Pretty sure. When you've been around long enough, you get an instinct."

"He's coming over," Abbie squeaked.

"Know him?"

"Yeah, but..."

"Want me to hang close?"

"Yes, please."

Wanda began an unrelated conversation as the man got close. "Better put the gloves back on, kid. That tall weed is a nasty one. Got these really fine spines that you can't see. If they get in you, they can get infected."

The man walked right into Wanda's personal space. "Take a hike."

She met his gaze. "I'm working here."

"Move it!" the man insisted. "I need to speak to my sister."

Wanda took a half step forward, putting the man off balance as he moved back. "Say what you like. I don't want to listen, but I don't like your attitude, and she is too young for you."

"You and I can hook up later, sweetheart, but what I have to say is private."

Wanda took two steps sideways and went back to work. She pretended not to be listening to the low intense, one-sided conversation. In fact, she didn't need to hear, when Abbie was broadcasting not only her discomfort of being near the guy, but her reactions to what he was saying.

Knowing that David had arrived and was close by, she decided to end the meeting and let David follow the guy.

She sub-vocalised into the mike. "Did you see the girl?"

She heard via the ear-bit, "She's look out. One of the uniform cars is about to drive by."

Aloud, Wanda said, "You gonna be all day? I ain't planning to do the rest by myself."

The man looked up, caught sight of the woman gesturing and

said, "Don't say I didn't warn you, Sis."

Abbie was pale faced as she turned around. Wanda read the signs and suggested, "You need to sit down and have a drink."
Abbie did, and Wanda asked, "You okay?"
"Yes," was the soft answer.
"Thought you didn't have sibs."
"I'm not sure they are."
"Want to talk about it? I'm not likely to ever see your folks."
"They said their dad is my dad, and that he ran out on them and their mum when they were young. Took all their mother's money, and even theirs from their bank accounts. Also said my dad married mum while he was still married to theirs."
"What do you think?"
"I don't want to think that, but Dad, he reckons someone is setting him up for trouble. He says he's done nothing illegal, but I think one of the teachers at my school also thinks he has."
"Did she actually say that to you?"
"No. She just said she'd like to talk to him, but it was when he was away on business."
Well, there it was, Wanda thought.

Abbie had confirmed most of what Annie had hinted at. There were still a couple of things.

"What do you think that brother of yours intends?"

"He says he's going to the police. That he has proof of bigamy and that he was into some scam years ago, under a different name."

"And you are afraid that if he goes to jail, you'll be destitute?"

"No. That he will take all his money and run," Abbie said.

"That's what I said," Wanda confirmed.

"He's already planning for me and mum to go to her cousin's place," Abbie went on. "Robbo says it's so we won't see he's going to run away."

"That's his name? Robbo what?"

"Mainwright, and his sister is Thea."

"How do you think your mother might react?"

"She'd say he'd never do it. That I'm his little girl and he'd not do that. And by the way he's been keeping me locked up, I don't think he'll dump me either."

"I think I missed a point there," Wanda commented.

"Well, I was looking for my birth certificate – while he was away. I thought I had found it in an envelope from the Births, deaths and marriages place. He had my name written on the envelope. But it wasn't. It was for someone else. I thought that meant I was adopted, but mum said I wasn't. My father was my father, but my mother was an old girlfriend who'd died but had said he was my father, so he took me in."

"So, whose certificate was it?" Wanda was suddenly hyper alert.

"Gabrielle Hartley."

With forced calmness, Wanda said, "I think I have heard that name somewhere."

"It's been in the papers. This old mad woman supposedly killed her daughters. One was Gabrielle Hartley."

Wanda heard an exclamation through her earbit, but Abbie hadn't finished.

"I think my dad wants to pass me off as her."

"That's a bit of a leap," Wanda told her, but her mind was suddenly busy. She was seeing a pattern that was so far only conjecture and spite.

"Look, kid. I don't know if you are right or wrong but if I was you, I'd talk to your Mum. Swear her to secrecy if you must, but warn her about what the guy said. She may not want to believe it, but tell her anyway."

"What if she won't listen?"

"You will have tried, and well, if you need help, I'll let you call me."

"Why? You don't even know me."

"I know what it is like to be 15 and living on the streets. And I'm not such a bitch that I'd not care if you ended up there."

Abbie burst into tears.

"Hey, kid. It may not come to the worst."

"If my dad goes to jail, my friends will dump me."

"Their loss. Dump them and make new ones. If they really are your friends, they will support you."

Abbie sniffled and hunted for a handkerchief.

Wanda suggested. "It's nearly lunchtime and I really need to find a ladies room. What about you?"

After emerging from the public toilets, they walked to the boathouse where lunch was to be provided. Abbie had splashed cold water on her face to wash the tears away. She went to the nearest bench seat and collapsed. Wanda went to the parks' supervisor and asked, "When do we finish up here?"

"You can go now if you don't want lunch. You just need us to sign you off."

"Great. I'll have lunch." She went back to Abbie and told her, then asked, "How are you getting home?"

"They usually send the housekeeper, but I'm in no rush. I'll stay for lunch."

Wanda grinned. "I thought you'd say that. Anyway, here." She passed a folded up piece of toilet paper to Abbie. It had her number on it. "Keep that safe or memorise it. You never asked, but my name is Wanda. And I meant what I said."

While she ate the pie she had opted for, Wanda listened through her earbit as David brought her up to date.

"We've found where those two are staying. A boarding house in Footscray. Robert and Thea Mainwright."

Wanda tapped the mike twice. Their signal for him to stop talking.

Abbie was asking, "What do you think I should do if that Robbo comes back and says I could go live with them, but I don't feel comfortable with them?"

"Kid, what I suggest is follow your instincts. But, if you have another option, you might be wise to take it."

"What are you saying? I hate it when mum and dad say one thing but mean another."

"Ok, I will be blunt. In my opinion, Robbo, and likely his sister, have done time. His body language is like that of ex-cons that I know. He may, genuinely, be concerned for you, but if your theory is correct and your father plans to use you for something, then Robbo could use you as leverage against him. To get money from him."

"I should tell my dad about him, but if I do it now, he'll be livid."

"Finish that drink, kid, and call your folks, and don't dislike being locked up."

That earned her a wry grin from Abbie.

David began speaking again when Wanda sub-vocalised an 'okay'.

"I warned Kelly that Carson might do a flit, but he says he's got nothing to justify a watch on him."

In a low voice, and with her head turned away from Abbie, Wanda said, "I'm thinking someone should watch Abbie Carson."

She didn't get an immediate answer, then, "Kelly says that since Robbo and Thea went home, she is probably safe enough going home."

Wanda had a sudden thought, and tapped the mike again.

"Abbie, where did you meet that guy in the first place?"

The girl didn't have to say anything, the memory of the meeting was blasted at her. Wanda saw it clearly, just as Annie had described. Abbie had gone white again.

"He and his sister broke into the house when Mum and Dad were away. They were searching dad's office. And I'm sure I'd put the alarm on. You know, I really think I do want to go up north."

Wanda refrained from asking 'where', since she sensed that Abbie didn't know. She also sensed that she had never heard of any such relatives.

In her ear, Wanda heard David say, "Can you keep her there? Kelly's on his way to follow her home."

She spoke softly into her microphone. "Will try."

Her intent was thwarted when a well-dressed woman came over and Abbie jumped up to meet her. Wanda reminded her to sign off, just after the woman had said, "Come on. Your Dad is waiting."

Abbie was hustled off, before she could try to introduce her new friend to her mother. She did glance back, and Wanda just grinned and put a finger to her lips. Abbie smiled back and returned her attention to where she was going.

Wanda told David they were leaving, and she'd meet him shortly. She grinned at the park supervisor, pretended to get signed out, and sauntered towards the main road.

"Now, you listen to me, young lady," Carson said over his shoulder, as he pulled up outside the rural homestead. "I don't want you calling your friends, or mentioning where you are by any means. I have organised to have your schoolwork faxed to the post office, and for someone to pick it up and bring it out."

Abbie decided she needed to play meek. "Oh, thanks. I didn't want to get behind everyone else. I'd be bored stupid if I had nothing to do. Do they have internet here?"

She heard a slight huff, as if her father had been about to rant at her. "I don't know. Do you need it?"

Keeping to her plan of seeming meek, Abbie merely said, "Sometimes the teachers make us do research. I guess you want me to stay here, so it's the only way I would be able to do so. Or is there a library I could go to?"

"Just do what you can for now. This is only likely to be for a week or two."

"So, who lives here?" Abbie asked brightly, hoping that by changing the subject, she would continue to keep her father off balance.

"I told you dear," Victoria Carson broke in. "My cousin and grandmother."

"Okay. I forgot," Abbie shrugged. "Are we going in?"

In fact, Abbie was curious to meet these supposed relatives. All her life she had assumed that she had none. Her friends had grandparents, cousins, aunts and uncles and she had felt she was missing out. In any case, Abbie had decided that appearing obedient was a better way to find things out. From recent experience, she had worked out that her father was nicer when he thought everything was going as he planned. And even if she still hadn't forgiven him for a lot of things, appearing to have 'come to her senses' would lull him. But she wasn't so naïve anymore. She'd bide her time. In her own mind was the idea that her father would be leaving as soon as he could get away, and when he wasn't around, her mother tended to let things slip.

She grabbed her case and school backpack when her father got out to do the gentlemanly thing of carrying her mother's two cases.

The door opened and light spilled out. It had become dark during the drive. She had tried to keep track of where she was going, but all she really knew for sure was that they had crossed into New South Wales. Then her father had turned off onto back roads.

"Victoria!" a gravelly female voice greeted. "It's good to see you."

The woman, old and bent, accepted a hug. "Jeremy! How are you?"

"Good, Mrs Bystead. I'd like to introduce my daughter, Abigail."

Abbie felt herself being pulled forward and she put her case down. She smiled at the old woman, and recalled her mother saying she was sick and might die. She sure didn't look it. Okay, she was moving awkwardly, but her hug was firm.

"Abbie, such a pretty thing you are. Come in. I'll have my daughter show you your room. You must be tired out."

"Thank you. Yes, I am tired. Um, what do you like to be called?"

"Oh, you can call me Nan," the woman said, although it came out more like she actually meant, "If you have to call me anything."

"Nan," Abbie echoed. "I'm looking forward to getting to know you."

"Time for that in the morning, dearie. Ah, here's Heather now."

The old woman looked at the younger who had just come into the hall. "This is Abbie."

The newcomer looked older than her mother, and hardly gave Victoria a glance.

"Hi Abbie, I'll help you get settled. Then I will see what I can find for you to eat, okay?"

"Are you Mum's cousin?" Abbie asked.

"That's right, but you can call me Heather."

"I've never heard Mum mention you."

"I'm not surprised. Your mother decided she'd rather live in the city. Seems she's done okay for herself."

Abbie shrugged. "I guess so."

"Here. I guess it's not quite what you are used to."

"It will be fine," Abbie managed to say, then picked on one thing she could sound enthused about. "Oh, you've got a desk in here! I want to keep up with my school work. Dad said he didn't know if you had the internet here. Do you?"

"Not much use for it here, sorry. I've heard of it, and everyone seems to think we now have to do everything online, but I'm happy to do things the way we've always done them."

"Too bad," Abbie shrugged as if the matter wasn't a big deal. She didn't know what her father had said about her, or if these relatives were going to watch her and tell him what she did. "Um, I don't really think I want anything to eat. Dad stopped somewhere on the way here and we had takeaway. I probably only want some water. Where's the bathroom?"

Abbie returned to her room and began unpacking her bag. When Heather brought the bottle of water, she would think Abbie really was getting ready for bed.

"Can you tell Mum and Dad I'm turning in? I've had a really tiring day."

Heather smiled, and left, closing the door after her.

To add verisimilitude to her claim, Abbie changed into her two piece pyjamas, but she wasn't as tired as she had claimed. During the trip, she had dozed whilst listening to her iPod. What she hoped to do was creep out and listen to her elders talking. Somehow, she felt something wasn't what they wanted her to think. It seemed like her Nan, and Heather, were acting a part, but not putting the right emotion behind it. Though, she had to admit, they might be unsure how to treat her. Maybe they hadn't known about her until recently either.

Well acting or not, they didn't know her, and she was going to be acting. They could think her naïve, or if her father mentioned recent events, scared, cowed or something. As soon as her father left, she would try to hear what the women started chatting about. They would wait until they were alone.

The engine starting and the crunch of gravel, told her when her father left. She peeked out her window, just to be sure. The front door was shut, firmly, and the outside light went off.

"Soon," Abbie told herself, before pulling down the rustic patchwork bedspread and testing the mattress. She scowled. It felt as hard as the floor. Staying there was going to be worse penance than the gardening had been. With a sudden thought, she pulled out her phone and found the GPS app, then checked she had reception. She had.

"So that's where we are!" Abbie muttered to herself. "Thurgoona."

Then she checked how much data she had. She didn't have much, so she probably couldn't connect her laptop to it. Then she checked her total. "Damn him!" she cursed her father. She used to have heaps more data. "Bastard!" she added. He would probably have a way to check her phone activity too.

Just as she had thought, the women had gathered in the old fashioned lounge room. A chink of bottle on glass suggested they were having sherry or something. The sounds carried clearly to the place Abbie had found to stand. They were at the "How long are you going to stay" stage. Her mother repeated the week or so line, but she didn't sound so sure now.

The old woman snorted. "What trouble are you in now, Vickie?"

"No trouble. Jeremey has some problems at work, that's all."

"Don't give me that! You and I both know how he makes his money. I warned you about him. They will catch up with him one day, and he will drag you right down to the streets, my girl."

"NO! He's not doing anything illegal. It's just that one of his business rivals is threatening him."

"Someone caught him out?" the old woman persisted. "That girl his?"

"Yes."

"You'd be better off without him, unless he's still got all his money to himself?"

"He hasn't. He transferred a lot of it to me."

"Then you'd better transfer it somewhere else, right quick."

"Nan, he wouldn't leave me."

"You lost any sense you had? If he's scared of the police, he wouldn't want them grabbing it. If he decides to run off, he'll take it from you just like..."

Abbie head a sound like knuckles cracking. She became aware of a bloated feeling in her gut. Did she want to hear anymore?

The old woman went on, "You're nothing but window dressing, just like that girl. Did he say where she came from?"

"Some old girl friend who died."

"And he took her in? Just like that? After dumping the girl friend? He must think her worth something then. Has he ever opened up about his past?"

"I don't care what he did in the past! He loves me! He has always provided well for me. I don't want for anything."

"Dream on, little Vickie. He has you right conned."

Abbie turned and hurried back to her room, feeling as if she wanted to be sick. These people seemed to think her father a crook, a conman. The memory of her textiles teacher came back to her, and Annie Jamieson's weird comment. "Was he a crook?"

Perhaps it was just as well she and Mum were visiting here. Her father hadn't been fit company, and he'd not have to worry about them. Maybe her Mum would tell her more in the morning. Right then, she was tired enough to sleep, no matter what horrid thoughts were in her head.

Roosters! Actual roosters were making an almighty racket somewhere nearby. Abbie tried to bury her head deeper under the blankets, and go back to sleep. Only now, she wasn't so tired and the bed felt every bit as hard as she had thought it would be. It was only just light outside. She was never awake that early.

It seemed though that someone else was. She could smell something that was making her stomach growl with anticipation. Deciding not to care about the hour, she dressed quickly and trotted to the kitchen.

Nan was standing at the range top, flipping pancakes from a pan to a plate being held by a tall, lanky boy, a bit older than herself.

"This is Austin," Nan said when she spotted Abbie, hesitating in the door way. "He and his brother Harry help with the work around here. You want breakfast?"

"Yes. It smells really good."

"There's enough for a slip like you, though I expected you to want some fancy cereal like Vicky."

"Well, I usually have that, but hey, I'm sort of on holiday."

Nan grinned. "Well, you take a seat. Today I'll do for you and tomorrow, if you're up, you can help me cook." She must have seen Abbie's expression, for she added, "Or doesn't Jeremy Carson think his daughter needs to know how to look after herself?"

Abbie shrugged, not sure what to say. Her father had said once that they were rich enough to have someone cook for them.

"So what will you want to do today?"

"I don't know. I do have school work."

"It's Sunday," Austin said, with his mouth half full. "You don't do school on a Sunday."

"You're going to be working," Abbie guessed.

"Yeah, but them cows need milking. They don't know one day from another. Want to come and see how it's done?"

Abbie was glad Nan put a plate with four pancakes, fried tomatoes, mushrooms, onion and bacon in front of her. "I might still be eating after you're done," she said, hoping not to have to agree. *Milking?* She could imagine what Gail and Helen would say. And then there would be the smell...

"Do you have outdoor shoes?" Austin considered, "Cos you go outside around here you need them."

"I didn't know I'd need any," Abbie admitted.

"Did germy Carson not tell you where you were going?"

"It was quite short notice," Abby defended her father. She decided not to say that supposedly Nan had been at deaths door. She caught Nan frowning at Austin.

"So, what's your best subject at school?" Austin timed the question between adding food to his mouth.

"Maths."

Austin scowled. "Germy must be your old man. Mum said he could use figuring to convince you of anything."

"Why do you call him Germy?" Abby asked, puzzled. "He's

always clean and well dressed."

Nan answered. "Sour grapes. Jeremy Carson had all the girls around here hanging off him. Until he decided to take off with the prettiest one he could find."

"Mum?"

"Yes. She was always a flighty one too. They deserve each other. Now you eat up. You don't look like you've been eating properly."

The morning dragged. Abbie had tried reading, then listening to her music. She couldn't go online to watch her favourite shows, and hadn't brought her sketchbook to try designing fashionable clothes. Her mum seemed to be living up to the prediction of staying asleep until noon and everyone else, including Nan had vanished. Her father couldn't have found a worse dead end dump to confine her in. A convent boarding school would surely be better. If she ever wanted to leave home, maybe she should let Nan teach her about cooking. Annie knew enough to cook for her parents, and seemed to take it for granted. She was a charity case though. Her parents didn't have a house keeper to cook and clean and all.

Finally, Abbie went out onto the veranda that ran three quarters of the way around the house. From there, she could see where Austin was driving a tractor in a field. He wasn't too bad looking, really, and he'd been okay to talk with at breakfast, even if he did eat and talk at once. Her father would have had something nasty to say about that. She had a brief pang of guilt about Adam, but he wasn't here and she wasn't meant to see him anyway. Maybe she could get Austin to talk more about how her father used to be. That was an idea.

Abbie's phone rang when she was working her way through the set maths work. She'd been struggling until she'd seen that Annie had sent through her class notes. She immediately silenced the ring and checked the number. It wasn't any of her friends, but then they'd be at school at that hour. It wasn't Adam either. If it was, she wouldn't have answered it. Then it clicked. It was the number that had been on the piece of paper that Thea had left for her in the garden at home.

"Hello?" she answered tentatively.

"Hi, little sister. Just wanted to check that you were okay. Didn't see you go off to school today."

"Yeah, I'm okay."

"Daddy send you away, did he?"

"No, Mum's relative was very ill. We came to see her."

"Well, Robbo and I don't like what our old man has been up to yesterday and today."

"Oh? Did you get to talk to him?"

"We delivered our message. Now the lousy two timing bastard is trying to discredit us," Thea was almost snarling. "However, we are doing things the legal way and keeping an eye on him."

"So why call me?"

"We thought you ought to know that he's been taking lots of boxes from your house to a storage unit."

Abbie didn't know what to think. "He's probably got a reason," she finally suggested.

"Yeah. We think he's fixing things so that no one finds anything if he has to take off at a moment's notice."

"Mum says he wouldn't," Abbie countered, but she began to feel queasy.

"Well, don't say we didn't warn you," Thea said, before hanging up, just as someone knocked on the door.

"Come in," Abbie called, as she slipped her phone in her pocket. "Oh, hi Mum, what's up?"

"Heather is going to take me into town to see how it's changed. Want to come?"

"Yes, please!"

Victoria Carson smiled. "You can go back to your work, later. It's good that you've got into it already."

Abbie decided to refrain from saying, "What else is there to do?" Instead she said, "I'll just change my shoes and get my coat." She could hear the wind blowing outside, and knew it was chilly too.

"Oh, Mum? Can I get some money? I need to get some personal stuff. My period is due and I forgot to pack what I need."

"Sure, but I need to get to the bank first. So don't be long – we are going in by bus."

Bus? Daddy only let her take the bus to school and back, never anywhere else, and not even that since the new housekeeper started. Didn't these relatives even have a car? This really was a rustic backwater. Even the internet on her tablet was hit or miss.

"Okay, Mum," Abbie agreed, getting up at once. She grabbed her iPod, so she could listen to music on the way.

The bus rumbled to a stop where half a dozen strangers where loosely huddled under a shelter. Abbie watched as her mother had to buy two day passes, and everyone else just swiped a card across a sensor pad. She assumed they were the local equivalent of Melbourne's Myki cards. The thought crossed her mind as to whether the Melbourne travel cards would work here. She had credit on hers, from before she stopped busing to school. At least they found seats, and she could sit by the window while her mother and Heather chatted across the aisle.

As soon as the bus began moving, she slipped in the earbuds from her iPod and turned to watch out the window. She had not seen much of the scenery as they were arriving. What she saw made her glad she didn't actually live around there. Everything seemed old, under-maintained and dull.

The occasional person she saw was rough dressed, rough looking, and obviously used to being out in all weathers. The same could be said of the extra people who got on or off at the seemingly endless stops.

"You're doing the right thing, Vicky," Heather said, after they had first taken off. "Your Jeremy is a sly one."

"Heather, he's..."

"Okay, you trust him. It doesn't matter. This way, if he does come back for you, you can say you did it just in case there was real trouble."

Even though she was looking out the window, Abbie knew her mother had twisted to look at her. She began tapping her finger in a random rhythm so her mother would think the music was deafening her.

"You're right. I know something is bothering him, but he won't confide in me. I think it is related to a break-in we had at our place one night. The intruder only searched his office. Jeremy keeps all his business records there. He said they didn't find where he kept all his really important papers though. He is really paranoid about the possibility of identity theft."

"What?" Heather scoffed. "Who would want to pretend to be him?"

"Oh, no. It's not like that. There are scammers who would try to get your private details and use them to clear out your bank accounts or obtain credit cards and run up huge bills on them."

"They wouldn't get much from anyone around here," Heather snorted.

Their talk turned to other things, giving Abbie a chance to think. He had their passports and family certificates in a plain box marked 'family'. Anyone rifling the place would have found them. Had found them, she corrected herself.

So what would he consider 'important' papers? Someone could open a bank account or get a passport with someone's birth certificate and passport. A small voice added, *and a medicare card and learner's permit.*

Two seats ahead, two men began chuckling loudly over some anecdote about a mate who had got drunk and been locked up for the night. Abbie tried to focus her ears back on Heather and her mother.

"Heard anything from him since he left?" Heather asked.

"Of course. He let me know he'd got home safely. He couldn't talk long, because he had an appointment with his lawyer."

Abbie smiled to herself, wondering if he had set the law on Robbo and Thea for annoying him. Maybe. But if their claims were bogus, why did he need to remove boxes of stuff? That suggested he had things to hide. Or was he simply worried about his reputation?

The conversation moved on again, and the topics were cryptic. Her mother and her cousin seemed to be referring to things they both knew about, and so didn't need to explain.

Abbie still hadn't turned her music on, because she was finding the new local culture mildly interesting. It was so different to that in Melbourne's inner suburbs.

Three quarters of an hour later, the bus stopped in town. Heather guided them to the central Commonwealth Bank branch.

Before she went in, Victoria Carson said to Abbie, "I'll transfer two hundred dollars into your account. Will that be enough?"

"Plenty, Mum," Abbie said, surprised. "I don't need to buy much, but I could use a better pair of shoes to walk around the farm in."

Heather laughed, "Vicky, go and do what you have to. I'll meet you back here in an hour. I can show Abbie where to go to get what she needs."

Victoria agreed readily. She liked shopping, particularly when she was buying for herself, not so much otherwise.

"Okay? Where first?" Heather asked.

"Um, I need stuff for my monthlies," Abbie said, feeling embarrassed to even mention it. Her mother didn't discuss such things, and it had been the old housekeeper who had taught her about them. "And I need some different shoes."

"Easy. Didn't Jeremy tell you where you were going?"

"Oh, Yes. But he didn't say it was like a farm." She sensed the confirmation of Nan's words that Heather didn't like her father. "Don't you like my dad?"

Heather seemed to stumble slightly, then laughed. "I'm probably just a bit jealous of Vicky still. She met him when he was staying in town, and decided to follow him down south. I told her she was a fool. A slick city guy like that wouldn't like one that was straight out of back of nowhere. Seems I was wrong."

"Would you want to live in a city?"

"Not really. I like the stars more than the city's bright lights. Vicky though, she liked the lights."

"So Mum grew up here?" Abbie asked, even though the answer seemed obvious.

"Didn't she ever tell you? "

Abbie shook her head, and Heather sighed.

"Well, that's one thing I don't like your Dad for. Once Vicky met up with him, she never looked back here. Never rang, never wrote, until, out of the blue, she rings and says she's coming for a visit."

Abbie had figured the latter was the case so artfully said, "Well, I'm glad I came. I needed a break from school."

"I was hearing things from Vicky. And if you don't mind me saying, you were lucky."

"I guess." Abbie didn't want to discuss that. "What was Mum like, growing up?"

Heather didn't answer right away. Then she said, "I'm not sure Jeremy would want you to know all that. He's obviously looking after you and Vicky. Giving you everything you want."

An imp of perversity caused Abbie to promise, "I won't tell Mum or Dad."

It seemed to be exactly what Heather was hoping. "Well, I guess," she made it seem she was reluctant, but quickly went on, "I should tell you that your Mum and I aren't really related, nor either of us to Nan. We were both as good as orphans. Nan took us in, so we got to be like sisters."

Abbie listened, fascinated. She was sorry when they arrived at the supermarket. Her mother, had been in and out of worse trouble than she herself had managed. Her mother had been the kind of person that her father touted as a 'bad' example, and of the types of people she was to avoid, when he emphasised, 'image' and 'like needs to seek like' – only that had backfired since he'd told her to befriend Gail, Helen and Jackie. Did he really not see that when he'd blamed her for the fiasco at school? When they had introduced her to the 'wrong sort of guys'?

Well, it probably wasn't surprising as to why her mother had cut ties with her past.

Abbie enjoyed shopping with Heather. She had a better sense of 'value' than her mother, and didn't question why she wanted to get new jeans as well as the shoes. Then, when Abbie came to an Optus store, and said, "I need to go in there. I want to see if I can get more data on my phone," she merely shrugged.

"Don't ask me to help you with that stuff, girl. You go and talk techy stuff and I'll be in the bookshop. But don't be long, we will need to get back to the bank to meet Vicky."

"Okay."

It didn't take long. The man in the store listened to her created tale of woe, about needing to get a cheap prepaid phone because she broke hers, and needed something until she got home.

It was easy. As there was no contract, she just had to give her details and pay for it. She declined any accessories other than the charger, and asked the man to help her set it up.

It had been a spur of the moment thing, since the shop had reminded her of how mean her father had been, dropping her data allowance right down and wiping her friends numbers from her phone before giving her the new one. Now she had a hundred times the amount of data, and could call who she liked and her father wouldn't know if he decided to check. And this was with Optus, not Telstra.

She'd left the box and packaging with the man, and the charger she slipped into the bag with her jeans. There would be no obvious evidence for her mum to see.

She probably wouldn't have done it if her mother hadn't said about putting more money into her account. The phone and the $50 credit for it had taken most of what she knew she had in her account.

They went a different way back to the bank, going past where the interstate buses came in. There was one headed for Melbourne, looking as if it would leave soon.

Victoria insisted on having a light lunch at an expensive looking café. Abbie didn't mind, she was already starving, but she saw Heather's mouth twitch. She was dressed up, compared to her usual attire, but still looked out of place there. A fact made obvious when the waitress automatically addressed Victoria.

"Still a stuck up bitch," Heather said quietly to Victoria, as she shrugged in the direction the waitress had gone.

"Who was that?" Victoria asked.

"Paula Green. You'd remember her from dance class. Of course, she's married now to the guy who owns this place, but a waitress is still a waitress. Not like you. I bet she doesn't even recognise you. I'd keep it that way."

That was all it took for her mother to become every bit as aristocratic as Jeremy Carson must have taught her. The waitress was a snob, ignoring Heather and a few others like her who had braved the café entrance.

By the time they were back at the farm, Abbie was exhausted. She decided to change into her new jeans and relax until tea time. She felt for the new phone in her pocket and grinned. Who could she call? Gail? Helen? Claire?

Somehow, even though they'd all be home from school by now, she dreaded facing their petty inquisition. Still, she knew their numbers well enough to program them into memory, and added others from memory or the list she had written down in her school diary. She added Annie's number, even though she didn't expect to have a reason to call her. Then she hesitated, and finally added the number Thea had given her.

Episode 11

The Tip of the Iceberg

<u>Chapter 1</u>

Annie saw the man accost Martin, but had to stay where she was. She was in the next group to compete in the 100m sprint. She saw Martin try to shake him off, but the old guy was persistent. She was in two minds about telling a teacher, but the nearest one was Gill, and he didn't like Martin.

Then it was time for the run. As she prepared to take off, she forgot all externals except for the need for speed. Only when she reached the finish line, being narrowly beaten by a leggy girl of Kenyan stock, did she think of Martin again. However, the teacher called over the first three place getters, and then she realised that she had just beaten Gail.

"Not a bad run, Charity Case," Gail praised, while simultaneously being insulting. "I thought I was sure to win with Carson being a no show. What else are you in?"

"The 200 metres, the 100 m hurdles and I thought I might try shot putt."

"Well, I will be ready for you in the 200," Gail warned.

"Go for it," Annie challenged.

"Are you only trying the shot putt to impress druggie Kemple?"

"Huh? Is that his thing?" Annie asked, with an innocent tone.

Even as they spoke, the PA was calling up the U16 boys for shot putt. She grinned at Gail, and went back to the seating to find her bag for a drink. On the way, she kept her eye out for Martin.

Martin felt his arm grabbed and instinctively jerked it. He turned, expecting his cousins. He wasn't expecting to see his father.

"How come you're out, you old bastard?"

"On bail, boy. I need your help."

"No way! There's a restraining order on you. You shouldn't even be here, let alone talking to me. And keep away from the house too, or you will be locked up again."

"Aw, boy, what are you being like that for?"

Martin just stared at him.

"Okay, Okay. But I just need somewhere to stay for a day or two."

"No! No! No! And if you try to get in and damage anything, I will have you hauled off."

"You're a right piece of shit, you know?"

"I learnt it from you, so get lost."

"Look, I'll stay somewhere else, okay, but I still need your help."

"I'm not lending you money, either."

"It's not that! I need to get a message to Gilroy."

"No way. He hates me too! Probably because of you! No way!"

"Get your cousins to pass on a message. I saw them before."

Martin considered that. It would be worth it if the bastard left him alone. "What message?"

"Just that I have some info for him."

"Okay, so get lost."

"What about my stuff?"

"I'll ring the local cops and make an appointment."

"What do you mean?"

"You aren't meant to be anywhere near me. That way, I can tell them you were and they'll put you back inside."

Martin had heard the call up for his event, and shook himself free of his father and began to stride off.

"You make sure to pass the message, boy!"

"I'll pass it, but I can't guarantee delivery. I'm busy for the next half hour, and the cousins are apt to take off early. Don't blame me for you being a snivelling coward."

"You'll get yours, boy."

"You hope! I know Gilroy hates your guts. He must have done quite a job on you — or you were so desperate for him to set you up for a murder charge."

"I haven't killed anyone. That was Mickey."

"That won't help you."

Martin heard the second call and took off at a run. He caught sight of Annie looking for him. She was frowning, but smiled when she saw him. He altered course to pass near her. He had reasons not to hang out with her at school, but this time he hoped she could help him. He gestured to the section of the field with the shotput nets, and was relieved when she began to trot after him.

When she caught up, and that surprised him, he heard her say, "Gill's on the rampage. He saw that bloke."

"Hope he calls the police. I would but I don't have my phone here."

"Nor do I. I left it back in my locker."

"Damn. Listen. That guy was my father. He's out on bail. He says he has info for my cousin's step-dad. I am supposed to give a message to the two morons to pass on."

"What info?"

"He didn't say. Can you go tell Gill that I need to talk to him?"

"You sure?"

"No, but he is sure to have a phone."

"OK, he was here, but he got another teacher to take over. I'll look for him. And anyway, good luck!"

Annie had wanted to see how shot putt was done. It had been an act of idiocy when she put her name down for it. Still, Martin was a good friend, and nothing like people thought. Asking her help meant he trusted her as well as liked her.

So, she'd look for Gill. He'd sounded severe enough when

asking her where Martin was. Obviously, he hadn't looked where she had and seen him and his father...or had he?

Would he have gone off to call the police? Or somewhere quieter to use his mobile phone?

Her feet took her past the grandstand, where the students could sit down and dump their bags. Further along was the clubroom cum office and canteen. She saw a teacher come out. Maybe Gill was in there.

Standing idly outside, in the uniform of a council ground keeper, was a short slender figure she recognised with relief. Wanda merely caught her look and shook her head.

Curious, but taking the hint, she went to the door of the clubroom and asked the teacher standing there if she could talk to Gill.

He came out with a frown that deepened when he recognised her. "Miss Jamieson, what brings you here?"

She repeated Martin's request, then added, "He'd have come himself, but he's just doing the shot putt heat."

"As it happens, I have already reported the incident," Gill said pompously.

"He hoped you would," Annie blurted. "He said the guy was his father, who was meant to keep away from him."

Gill's expression eased. "Thank you, Miss Jamieson. I'll take the matter from here."

"Thanks, Sir," Annie told him before turning to go back and watch Martin. She glanced sideways at where Wanda had been, but she was gone.

The question of why Wanda had been there, and gone, occupied her until she caught up with Naomi and began to compare results.

<u>Chapter 2</u>

That someone had bailed Kevin Kemple wasn't a complete surprise. Kelso, via his former protégé, knew as soon as the bail intermediary had got in touch with the authorities. Word had gone back to slow the process as much as possible so someone could be put in place to follow Kemple.

He and Delaney had been kept apart in the remand prison, but she knew how messages could still be sent. So whilst David was still trying to trace the money trail, related to the prototype device, she got to follow Kemple. Her back up was Kelso's assistant Fred.

They'd arrived as Kemple was being led out the gates, and watched from a distance away. No one was there to meet him, for he walked to the nearest bus stop, which ran between Sunshine and Laverton railway stations. Fred followed the bus to Laverton station, and dropped Wanda off to follow him on the train back to Melbourne. He never noticed her, although he kept looking around – possibly for his unexpected benefactor.

In the city, he changed platforms, and as he waited, Kemple made calls on his mobile phone. He paced as he spoke, and slammed the flip phone shut when it ended unsatisfactorily. Finally, he must have got the answer he wanted, for he stalked back to the large display board with the departure times and made for a particular platform. Wanda had no trouble blending into the crowd and boarding the same train. After getting off at Victoria Park, he made a beeline for a sports ground where a school was having its sports day. He had used a taxi for the short trip, but Wanda had met up with Fred who she'd told the train's destination. Wanda realised that the school was that which Annie and Martin went to, as some students were in ordinary school uniform, not sports uniform.

She pondered the question of who he had called, and if he had wanted to know where the school kids were.

Wanda had not been able to get close when Kemple had accosted his son. She had been warned that hanging around a school event wasn't a good idea – but at least it wasn't on school grounds, and she had found a dropped groundsman's shirt and put it on.

She had already noticed Annie being quizzed by a teacher who had also noticed the Kemples together. She'd followed the teacher, just on a hunch. Likely the school had been warned Kemple was out.

The canteen was, she guessed, the teachers' rest room for when they were having a break from supervising. By listening at the window, she heard what Annie had told him. She had already identified him as Gill, from his description and attitude. She waited, even though the conversation died down, and was rewarded by seeing Annie coming to the canteen.

She shook her head to tell Annie not to notice her, and the girl was quick on the uptake, but her voice was just loud enough to carry. It told her more than she had expected, and sent her hurrying back to where Fred had been waiting in the car.

She arrived to see his blue ford turning a corner, down the road. She turned to go the other way where there was a bus stop. She hadn't gone far when she had the sudden sense that she was being watched. She continued at a casual pace, and then feigned twisting her ankle on a piece of broken footpath. Limping to where she could lean against a brick fence pillar, she pretended to feel her ankle as she checked both ways along the street. She memorised the people she saw, then limping still, she continued onto the bus stop and pretended to scan the timetable and casually turned to check each way along the street again.

A tall, lithe, dark haired man in dark slacks and jumper ambled her way. His face was familiar, and it didn't take long to identify him. Stephan Tatarovich, who was her maternal uncle, and who should have still been in an Austrian prison. Did she want to greet him? No!

Wanda saw a taxi approaching and put her hand out to hail it. The taxi swerved to the curb and she got in, telling him to go to Hawthorn station. She had a glimpse of the scowl on her uncle's face as the taxi moved off. Did he know who she was?

Wanda sent a text message to David and his reply, not unexpectedly, was, "Get back here, now!"

Kelso listened to her report, and in turn told her that Kemple had found a coffee shop and seemed to be intending to stay there. He went on to say, "What I would like to know is what is so urgent for Kemple to tell Gilroy. Or is the message from Delaney?"

David put in, "I'd like to know why The Family had someone tailing Kemple."

"There was no one else watching when he got out," Wanda said with assurance. "But he was making a lot of calls before he headed to the sport ground."

"Okay, so assume those Russian bastards heard that Kemple was out," David suggested. "I know they would not be happy that Delaney was caught and we got the device back. Assume also that Delaney knew or heard something to suggest that they would come after him. Also assume, that Delaney could have got a message to Kemple even if they were supposedly kept apart. Do you think Stephan heard what Kemple was saying to Martin?"

"I wasn't that close, and Kemple had gone before I heard what I did. Assume it is possible. I wasn't expecting to see Stephan at all! And I only had the sense of being watched after Kemple had gone off in the taxi," Wanda specified.

"Do you think he noticed your interest in Kemple?" Kelso inserted.

Wanda considered that. "I would have to say it was possible, even if Kemple and I both arrived separately. I don't know where he came from."

David had a more urgent question. "Do you think he recognised you?"

"I didn't get that feeling," Wanda told him. "Besides, I've changed a lot and I don't think his memory is as good as mine. Or that he would conceive of meeting me here."

"Okay, forget all that for now," Kelso went on. "How might Delaney do damage control? What could he say to fend off the wrath of the Family? What might he have to bargain with?"

"The next best thing to having the device itself, would be to have the specs and technical data," David proposed. "Were they with the device when it was stolen?"

Kelso stiffened. He rose and went to where a file binder was shelved. After retrieving it, he checked several pages.

"All this says is that the device was in a special box, for transport. We haven't found the box – since the device was loose when you retrieved it. I will ask about the specs, they may have been in the box, or they may have been sent separately."

"I could re-check Kemple's garage," Wanda offered.

"No!" Kelso and David said together.

"Okay, no need to be narky," Wanda told them. David let Kelso give the reason for not re-checking Kemple's garage.

"Now you have identified your Russian relative, and we know of their interest in Kemple – you need to keep right away from Kemple, Gilroy, and ideally Kemple's son. I will suggest to Des that Kemple's garage be checked again. The local boys can do it."

"And you will contact Interpol? I thought Stephan and Leo were meant to be in prison," Wanda suggested. She saw David's fierce grin.

Kelso nodded. "I think you should concentrate on helping Maude Hartley."

"On that," Wanda asked, "Are you going to question Mickey Delany again?"

"No. Homicide will take him on. I doubt he would tell you anything anyway."

"Tell, no," Wanda agreed, "but I might be able to get impressions from him."

"I don't have any authority to interfere in current local investigations," Kelso sighed. "Anyway, Delaney won't be going anywhere. Des believes they have a good case against him for the murder of the guard."

"Okay, he'll keep. And I doubt he'd willingly tell me what he did with Maude's kids. However, have you forgotten that Delaney and possibly Carson are both involved with Maude?"

"We haven't any real proof against Carson," David reminded her.

"Yet!" Wanda promised. "My gut is telling me that he is up to something shady, even if not this."

Kelso reached for an envelope that had been sitting on his desk. "This came from Des earlier. I was waiting for you to get back to open it."

In one of those 'just knowing' moments she often got, Wanda paled. "The DNA results? What did Des tell you?"

Instead of answering, Kelso slit the envelope open and took out the photocopied sheets. He glanced at the cover page, as if confirming what he had been told, then passed them to her. David stood and came to look over her shoulder.

Now used to looking at official reports, she went from the blunt conclusion that the DNA of the dead little girl buried behind the scout house matched that of the hair sample of Danielle Hartley, to look at the raw results. It felt like someone had just given her a gut punch. The dead child had been little older than her own daughter.

Then she read the report, completely. The DNA had come from some hairs caught up in the fastening of the dress the child had died in. She recalled the post mortem report that had said all the child's hair had rotted away.

"I'm going to go over everything you have on Delaney and Carson," Wanda stated. "And the finds at the house."

"I have spoken to Maude's Trustees. Tyrell is aware of what's in the report," Kelso told his assistants. "I also have the report back from the interview with Carson's previous housekeeper."

"Anything useful?" David asked.

"Not a lot," Kelso summarised. "She went to work for Carson after he got married and before the child came. Her recollection of that day was that he turned up with her, said she was his and the mother was dead. The child herself kept crying for someone else for a while. She said Carson was a good employer. When he and his wife went off for business, she stayed at the house to mind the child. He paid her extra at those times. This time, he just assumed she was available and can't have got her message. She was a bit angry at the abrupt dismissal, but she does now have to care for her mother."

"What about odd visitors?" Wanda asked.

"She didn't recognise those two who claimed to be Carson's kids," Kelso told them, "But she thinks that Mickey Delaney came to the house. She didn't open the door because she didn't like the look of him when she checked through the spyhole. She said Carson was very particular who he let into the house."

"When was that?"

"Probably within days of Delaney being released."

"Now that is interesting," Wanda murmured. Her earlier comment had been pure speculation. Now her mind was concocting reasons for Mickey Delaney to make a beeline for Carson.

David distracted her. "Are they going to tell Maude about the results?"

Kelso nodded curtly, but didn't miss Wanda's sudden tensing. "At least she will know…"

"Well, if Maude wants me, I am available," Wanda promised. Then she blurted, "Is it possible to get hold of child protection information from twelve years ago?"

"What is your reasoning?" Kelso asked.

"Nothing specific, yet. Just questions in my mind."

"Try them on me?" Kelso invited.

"Okay. Two girls were taken off Maude, with Delaney's connivance. Now, before you say that one died, I have seen Maude's memory of that time. Both were alive, although one seemed clingy, so may have been unwell. They both had to have gone somewhere. Now, it seems, one ended up buried in Maude's garden. And possibly, Carson picked up the other. How long after they were taken, did he do that? And if the people who took them told him of one girl, why not the other? If one girl was sick and died, why would she be buried in secret in that garden? Is that allowed here? And, next time I talk to Maude, I want to see if she recalls what her girls were wearing when they went away? That little girl in the garden was dressed in a party dress. It might meant that at sometime, some other kid's outfits were taken from Maude's place."

Kelso considered her insights. He knew of her special abilities, although he could not use them as evidence. "I will talk to Des about trying to get access to the Department of Human Services records and let him suggest some of the other ideas to the Homicide team."

"Okay, I'll get onto reviewing those reports," Wanda agreed. "I want all the info lined up in my memory."

"I didn't think you would need to review it," David teased.

"I may not have seen all that's available," Wanda retorted. "The more we know, the more likely we can spot lies."

Kelso made another suggestion. "Maybe you should go and see those two who claim to be Carson's earlier children. Des said that he got a restraining order out on them."

"Maybe I should," Wanda thought aloud. "What caused that? Did you hear?"

Kelso chuckled. "They had him served with papers for eight years default of child support, and for bigamy. They claim his marriage to Victoria was illegal as he was still married to their mother at the time."

"So, Carson has tried to gag them. They won't be allowed to contact him, but I don't think that will stop them."

"No, but they will have to be careful," Kelso commented.

"The question is...what to tell them as to how I found them, when they think me some petty delinquent."

Kelso didn't answer, for just then, Wanda's phone rang, and so did David's.

"Hi Annie. What's up?" Wanda answered.

David had answered his phone, giving his caller short answers. When he saw Wanda's raised brows and guessed her tacit question, mouthed, "Tyrell."

<u>Chapter 4</u>
(Annie POV)

"So you came fourth in shot putt and second in the 100m," Martin summarised. "Not bad. What about the 200m?"

"First!" I couldn't help grinning. "And was Gail furious. She thought that with Abbie not being there, she'd have it easy."

"She's out of condition," Martin commented.

"So? How did you go?" I hadn't seen Martin since the trials to find out.

"First!" His grin was huge. "Did a personal best, too."

"Your father must have really aggravated you."

"You been touching my stuff?" Martin suddenly challenged.

"No, but I figured it was obvious. Oh, guess who else I saw? "

"Who?"

"Wanda. I think she went off after your dad. I think she was listening when I gave Gill your message."

"I wonder why that pack of shit interests her."

"Might still be about that business in the park."

"Yeah, I guess. Anyway, I hoped he'd stay locked up. Wonder who paid his bail."

"He must have some friends," I suggested.

Martin shrugged. "He told me he had a message for the cousins' step-dad. I'm supposed to tell them to pass the message on. Trouble is, those two cretins managed to lose themselves this arvo."

"Don't they usually ride home this way?"

"Not always. Less so since you faced off Gerry."

"They're just petty bullies," I told him. "What was the message?"

"He didn't say and I didn't ask. It was just that he needed to talk to the cousin's stepfather. Which is weird, since Gilroy hates his guts."

"Was he being held with Mickey Delaney?"

Martin shrugged. "Think the message was from him?"

It was my turn to shrug.

"I said I'd pass that message just to get rid of him and told him of the restraining order. If he wants his stuff, he can call the police."

There didn't seem anything more to say about that, so we walked in silence. We were both tired from being outside all day. My phone pinged a message, and as I was replying, Martin muttered, "Talk of the devil."

I heard the sound of bikes coming up behind us and glanced over my shoulder.

"Hi, runt," Tom called. "Heard Gill was on the warpath, wanting to see you. Did you almost hit him with that last shot you put?"

"Nah, I missed the bastard," Martin shrugged. "Anyway, I saw him, talked to him and got away unscathed. Is that why you two nicked off?"

"We left because we were bored. Why was Gill on your back?"

"Not mine. He saw my old man at the venue," Martin said. He took the opportunity to pass on the message. "The old man wanted me to pass onto you a message for your step-daddy."

"What message," Gerry snarled.

"The old goat didn't say," Martin stared at his cousin.

"Where will he be?" Tom demanded.

"Who cares," Martin shrugged. "He didn't say, and anyway I figure he expected your step-daddy to know where to find him. Likely he's into all the criminal haunts."

Tom looked to be about to take a swing at Martin, who hopped backwards and Tom fell off his bike. Gerry didn't try to emulate his brother. "The step-dad is hell on criminals. That's why he hates you and your old man."

"Then he must really have torn into you two when you got

mixed up with Tory Michaelson," I had to say.

"Shut your mouth," Tom snarled at me as he got back on his bike. He turned to Martin, "Why should we pass the message on?"

"Personally, I don't care if you don't. I had the feeling the information was time sensitive, and maybe that means my old man will miss out on something. Or, maybe yours will. Do you want to be the cause of that?"

The twins rode off without a further word. Martin mused, "Something has them in a foul mood. I apologise for being related to them."

"You couldn't help that and I don't have to like them."

"Yeah, well..."

"Naomi just texted me. The police have been over the scout place with a fine comb and have said they are finished there."

"I don't suppose they mentioned the outcome of anything they found?"

"She didn't say, but I doubt it."

"I wonder if Wanda or David will tell us anything."

"Only what they are allowed to," I had to say. "I might text her later and see if she will tell us anything. I would like to know if they identified the kid they found."

"What about the other stuff?" Martin asked.

I felt myself shudder as I thought of those things. "Yes and no."

I was glad when he dropped the subject.

When I got home, after playing with Lucky-pup, having a shower and starting to get tea ready, I had forgotten about texting Wanda. I remembered after tea, when I was trying unsuccessfully to work on an assignment. I decided it was a good reason to stop, but I didn't get an immediate answer. I shouldn't have expected one.

But that made me think of the rest of Maude's stuff, and what Wanda had suggested to try to control what I picked up. She said I had to keep practicing the ideas to make them automatic.

Okay, I told myself, *I am wearing cotton gloves – they will keep off dust, but may let moisture in.*

Most of what was left looked like tawdry bric-a-brac, and I was relieved to feel very little from most of the things.

When I had emptied the box out, I had several crocheted doilies done in fine cotton, but now stained and dirty, a book mark memento of someone's funeral, some cheap toys from show bags or McDonald's, (all from one of the Disney movies), some folded drawings that her girls might have done, an old watch that didn't work, an old, empty make up compact, a pair of glasses, an old instamatic film camera, a couple of beaded necklaces and a leather wallet.

Little enough to indicate someone's life.

I told my mind that my hands were bare, and had a closer look at the wallet. No visions came to me, but then, it had been in that house, tossed aside like rubbish, for a long time. I checked all the compartments – no money, or ATM cards, or personal ID. On the outside, the stitching was rotting away, part of the inside was visible, something creamy brown, probably cardboard to strengthen the wallet. I was curious though, and went to get the tweezers from my make-up set to ease it out. It was actually paper, folded over and over. I poked with the tweezers again, and found where an inner seam had given way. Why had the owner slipped the paper in there?

I opened the paper carefully. The ink had faded, but I could just make out a string of symbols and numbers, but they made no sense to me. I put that into a clean envelope, but before I closed it, I put a finger lightly on the paper.

The vision that came was intense, I saw a hand holding an old style floppy disc, and a computer screen full of a spreadsheet, felt a sudden extreme terror, and a need to hurry, close the program, and to hide the password. Then, oddly, as time rolled back, a strong sense of elation.

The flash gave me no idea of the location, and before the details faded, I began scribbling them into my vision quest diary. This wasn't one of Maude's memories, it had a different feel. I examined the wallet again, but there was still nothing to give me more clues. I put the wallet aside and checked the watch. It looked to be a man's watch.

Again, there was no immediate flash. I had found this pushed to the back of a makeshift drawer. On the back it had, *To Charles from Felicity*. The first person that came to mind was Charles Hartley. I couldn't prove that, but I wrote down the wording of the inscription and my guess, but with a question mark. I included a description of the watch, thinking Maude might like the watch back.

The camera was the last thing I wanted to try. It was like one I'd had as a kid before digital cameras had come into fashion. There was a film in it, seemingly unused, from the frame counter. That surprised me. But maybe the police had removed one from it and replaced it with a new one.

I decided that was enough, and began putting things back. I hadn't reinforced the glove idea on my mind, so when I touched the bookmark again, the intensity caught me by surprise. Grief so powerful that I wanted to cry.

I brushed tears away and read the front of the narrow card. "Timothy Hartley, Mar 1985 to July 1985".

I swore. Somehow, I knew that the child had been Maude's.

How had the baby died? Poor Maude, perhaps it wasn't so surprising that she'd gone funny when her girls were taken.

After that, I needed to talk to someone. I wished I could talk to Mum, but she would tell me not to imagine such unpleasant things. So I tried Wanda's number.

"Wanda?" I asked when the phone was answered.

"Hi Annie. What's up?" the familiar voice reassured me.

"I found something amongst that stuff of Maude's that I collected for her at the house."

"Oh?"

"Yes. It's one of those cards people give out at funerals, or rather this is like a book mark. But, it's for a Timothy Hartley. He died in 1985, but he was only three or four months old. Do you think Maude was his mother?"

"Well, her brothers were dead before then," Wanda told her. "Look, I will try to find out. Was there something else?"

It sounded like Wanda had other things on her mind, but I had to ask, "Have they identified that second kid's body yet?"

I thought the line had cut out then, but finally Wanda said, "Yes."

"Was...was it one of Maude's?"

"It seems so," Wanda said softly. "But it is not for the public yet."

"Oh! Poor Maude. Will they give her a hard time?"

"I don't think so."

Wanda sounded like she was hoping she was right.

"I want to visit her. Do you think that will be allowed?"

"Have you asked your folks?"

"Not yet, but Naomi said she'd come with me." I mentally crossed my fingers. She had offered, but I hadn't asked her yet.

"I can see if I can find out. Why do you want to go?"

"Well, to see if she wants to keep any of this stuff. And, well, she might like a friend."

"I think that's very kind of you, Annie. I'll get back to you."

Wanda ended her call and waited for her husband to finish his talk with Maude's trustee. She looked quizzically at him when he said, "Wanda's free now. I will put her on."

"Hello?" Then she listened.

"Yes, I can go and see her this evening. Do you know what she wants? Have you heard the results of the DNA test? Does Maude know? How did she take it? Well, that's to be expected. Do you think she would like a visit from a couple of youngsters? Annie and her scout friend Naomi. I was thinking on Saturday. Okay, I will find out. And there was one other thing. Did Maude have a child before the girls? Yes, Timothy Hartley, died in 1985, aged 3m. Yes, thanks. I'll pass you back to David."

When Wanda had filled David and Kelso in on the other half of her conversation, she asked the former policeman, "The earlier DNA results, using the hair from those hair slides, do you have them?"

"The ones of Danielle and Gabrielle Hartley," David asked. "They should be with the other reports." He stirred himself to go and find them.

"Kelso, did the lab send a report from the comparison with the other twin's hair?"

"It wasn't a match, why?" Kelso answered.

Wanda didn't answer, she had taken the earlier DNA file from David and was reading it carefully. The summary page had simply said that Maude was definitely the mother of the twins, who were non-identical. Now she looked at the raw data, and something became glaringly obvious.

"Kelso, the twin girls are non-identical, but surely the DNA of both twins should be fairly close, wouldn't it?"

"The maternal DNA is," David pointed to that statement.

"Did they do a DNA scan of the boy victim they found?" Wanda asked.

"No, there was nothing they could use," Kelso explained.

"They only had bones."

"They can use bones," Wanda told him. "The preparation is different and it takes longer. Can't your lab do it?"

Kelso reached for the phone and dialled a number. David went and hooked up his laptop.

Kelso asked the question Wanda had voiced, and listened to the reply. He was about to hang up when Wanda asked, "Can you find out what this word means?"

The former policeman's brows rose into his hairline. He asked the question, listened then thanked the caller and hung up.

"The word relates to an uncommon situation where there has already been one egg fertilised in a woman, but then another egg and sperm join," Kelso managed to get the information out. "What are you referring to?"

"These results for the twins. Superfecundation! Maude's girls, had different fathers."

"That's impossible!" Kelso blurted.

"No," David refuted. "It's rare, but Maude must have had sex with two men on the same day, or at longest, on consecutive days."

"Well, how interesting is that. I wonder if Maude will tell us who they were. She didn't recognise Carson."

Wanda began to smirk. "If Carson is going to claim paternity, he obviously wasn't using the name Carson then. And wouldn't it be a shock, if the twin he thinks is his, actually isn't?"

"I certainly missed that data," Kelso said. "But, I think, that it should stay just between the three of us. I won't even be telling Des just yet. Now, what was that about not using the name Carson?"

"You recall, when Maude went into HQ that time? Carson came storming past us. Maude thought he looked familiar, but she didn't remember the name Carson?" Wanda saw Kelso nod, and went on. "Well, how do you read Maude? I don't think she would have been one to be going out and about and finding a casual one-night stand. She likes having sex, she said Mickey was good in bed. So I think, she agreed to have sex with the fathers of the girls, but I think they were both people she knew well, and probably trusted."

"Maude hasn't told anyone who the father of the girls was, not even her trustees," Kelso pointed out.

"If the act was consensual, what business of theirs was it? She was over eighteen, and probably was when she conceived the boy."

"What's your point?" Kelso growled.

"Maybe I should try to get her to name who she thinks is the father of her girls?" Wanda proposed. "If she names Carson, okay or if he comes forward, we'd have a reason to get a DNA sample from him."

"That's what you advised Tyrell, so what other use might you have for Carson's DNA? If we get permission, it will only be allowed to be used within well-defined parameters – if he is not being charged with a serious crime."

Wanda growled, but it was an admission of being caught out. "Perhaps to compare it with some from that Robbo and Thea."

David asked Kelso, "Have you, or your former colleagues done anything about checking Carson's background?"

"Some, but so far there is nothing against him, not even a parking ticket," Kelso told them. "We know he has lived in this area for at least 18 years and we have checked records with the banks and the tax office. He has bank records back forty years, and tax records for the past thirty years. Prior to that, looking at his bank accounts, he wasn't earning enough to pay tax."

"Well, he has certainly come up in the world. That house would have cost a lot," Wanda estimated.

"He rents it," Kelso corrected. "However, the point is valid. The rent would be quite high. What else are you thinking?"

"That, and about those two who claim him as a parent. If they are correct about him, and they are using their birth names, then Carson changed his name when he walked out on them. He didn't want to be found. Which would fit with their belief that he was a con artist. And, I estimate that when he came here it was just after he walked out on them, and if that is the case, he had a new identity ready to walk into."

"You said they spoke to Carson's daughter," Kelso remarked. "So, obviously they are aware of her. I think you were right, we should have kept an eye on her. When is she meant to be doing Community Service again?"

"Saturday," Wanda confirmed.

"I think you should warn her to keep away from those two. Do you have her number?"

"No, but she has mine."

"Tell me what Abbie Carson said about them," Kelso directed. Wanda did.

Kelso considered. "Thirty years...if the man is about your age, he'd have been born about then. Carson has records going back forty years – it tends to suggest that Carson isn't their father."

"He could have changed his name," Wanda said, but David corrected her.

"He would have had to have been living two identities," he insisted. "What kind of income did Carson have until he started to pay tax?"

Kelso checked a folder. "Regular payments in, and cash taken out. Low compared to the pay rates in those days."

"Abbie said, they said, their mother had inherited money, and he ran off with all of it," Wanda suggested. "Twenty years ago. I think we need to get those two in to talk about their father."

"We still don't have a solid reason to investigate Carson," Kelso reminded them.

Wanda growled in frustration. "If those two thought he had done something criminal, why didn't they report him to the police?"

"The statute of limitations would have run out by now," Kelso told her.

"And," David told her, "If he's in jail, they won't get any money out of him. They must think they have enough evidence of something on him to worry him."

"He will slip up," Wanda predicted. "Can I borrow Fred to drive me to Maude's community house?"

"Hello, Maude," Wanda greeted when she was led into the communal living room at the community house. Several of the other residents eyed her curiously, and she grinned back at them.

"Wanda, friend. You came."

"Of course." Wanda pulled a chair around and settled into it. "This place is nice."

"Friends here. Nice ones."

"Have you been practicing your sums?" Wanda asked. Then she tried a test, asking mentally, "Did you hear from the police?"

"Sums yes. Old time things too."

Wanda shrugged. It was too much to hope that the telepathy could go both ways. Or had she sort of sensed the question?

"Talk alone? You, me?"

"Okay," Wanda agreed. "Where?"

"Garden. Flowers there. Not too cold yet."

Wanda followed Maude, gave a wave to the receptionist who had let her in, and guessed the garden would be unoccupied. They settled again, this time on two wood and metal garden chairs.

"Need help," Maude began. "Say found my little Ellie. Found dead."

Wanda nodded, cautiously.

"Understand, I don't. Mickey had both taken. Together."

"Tell me about that time," Wanda suggested quietly. "Think it through."

"You see me thinking?"

"I will try to."

Wanda concentrated more on the thoughts going through Maude's head than on the stilted conversation. When Maude paused in her recollection, because the emotions were getting too strong, Wanda took out a small notebook and made some rapid notes – descriptions of people, clothing, and other things.

When Maude looked up at her, Wanda asked, "Did the people who came to take the girls, identify themselves? Or explain why they were taking them?"

"No. Mickey say I can't have them."

Wanda considered the memory she had shared. In it, Maude had seen a woman dressed as a nurse, and a man and woman in suits. Mickey had scooped one girl off the floor and given her to the nurse. The other woman had taken the other girl from Maude's lap. That girl had begun to shriek, and twist to get back to her mother.

Mickey, and the man, had held a distraught Maude from going after them. The memory ended abruptly, and Wanda suspected that the suited man, possibly a doctor, had sedated her.

One question Wanda had wanted answered was. The two girls had not been wearing pretty party dresses, but bib and brace style overalls.

"What did the police ask you?"

"How Ellie got in garden. Didn't know. Said so. Nasty they were. Say Mickey say, I did it."

"Last I heard, Mickey wasn't saying anything," Wanda murmured. "I wonder what he thinks he will get out of lying."

"You ask Mickey?"

Wanda gave a grunt. "I would love to get close enough to him to ask him questions, but they won't let me. Tell me something. When did Mickey make the garden? Before or after the girls were taken?”

“After. Mickey say, do it for me. Say ready when girls back.”

“How long after that, did they take you away?”

“Little time.”

Wanda sensed that Maude’s recollection of time was hazy. Either she had been kept drugged, or all her days merged together.

“So you wonder how Ellie got into the garden,” Wanda murmured, and Maude nodded.

“That is a very good question,” Wanda told her, having wondered that herself. “Did Mickey ever say who people were? The ones who took the girls?”

“Deep, Dep...”

“Department?” Wanda guessed.

“Yes, yes.”

“Then, surely he would have been given a way to get in touch with them. Would they have given him access?”

“What you think?” Maude asked Wanda.

“I don’t know what the procedures were back then. I would have assumed that the girls would be cared for until the doctors said you were okay. I believe that you had an accident just before that time.”

“Not accident.”

“Mickey?”

“He push me. Hit me. Put in hospital.”

“Did you tell police that?”

“Never asked. They think me...”

“Addled,” Wanda finished for her. “You probably were. I think Mickey was giving you stuff.”

“Think better when he not around.”

“Let’s talk about something else,” Wanda suggested.

Episode 12

Events Heat Up

Chapter 1

Wanda went on, "You said, Mickey said, Gabbie was still alive."

Maude nodded.

"Did he say anything else? Any other time?"

While Maude was thinking, Wanda made more notes.

"Just to do as say. Then take me. Ask when. Say when ready."

"Okay, just a silly question. Could Mickey tell the girls apart?"

"No. But they not alike."

"Yeah, but some people think 'twins- can't tell them apart.'"

Wanda wondered if she should ask Maude about the baby Annie had told her about. This might be the best time.

"Maude, I want to ask you something, and I hope you won't get upset. Did Mickey know about Timothy?"

Wanda reached out and took the older woman's hand when her eyes filled with tears.

"How you know?"

"Annie found a little card amongst the stuff she saved for you."

"Annie nice girl. No. Never told Mickey. My secret. Wanted little one for mum and pa."

Wanda waited, sensing more to come.

"Gerry died. Charlie died. Only me left. Pa wanted our name. Wanted me to marry Clay and keep name. Clay...he need better than me."

"Clay?" Wanda queried.

"Clay....ton" Maude forced out. "Liked him. Friend. He sad boy died."

There were many complex memories going through Maude's mind. Finally Wanda asked, "Did you let him go? Say you wouldn't marry him?"

Maude nodded, eyes still watering. "He need better than me."

"You are a very special person, Maude," Wanda said softly. "Have you kept in touch with him?"

A head shake was the answer until she said, "Saw him twice. Had letters for a while."

Maude's eyes became brighter, and she swiped at the tears. "He said, should have married me. Wife made him sad."

"When was that?" Wanda asked the question gently, but she already had a good idea.

"In bed. Clay gentle in bed."

"Is he the father of the girls?"

"Might be, but I said it was Wally."

"Wally?"

Maude nodded. "He from trusty place. Knew face. Came to say, sorry ma and pa died."

"He let me cry. He hug me, and....I wanted baby, for them."

"So Wally and you..." Wanda wasn't sure what words to use. "What was he like?"

A flood of sensations threatened to overcome Wanda. She had her mental shields way down. "Whoa! Okay, he was good in bed. What about his face? Manner?"

This brought more memories and some vivid mental images. Wanda memorised them. Maude didn't have the words to describe him.

"Looks rich," Wanda suggested, but she was thinking, *Deliberate gigolo.*

"Said he was."

"When were you together?"

"Day after Clay."

Wanda suddenly laughed, and Maude looked at her. "What funny?"

"Ah, do you recall those hair slides, you kept with the girl's hair?"
Maude nodded.
"They did a DNA test using hairs from them. Do you know what DNA is?"
"What makes person. They said they match hairs on ..."
"Yes, but that wasn't what I was going to say," Wanda told her. "In twins, the DNA in identical twins will be identical, or very similar in fraternal twins."
"Twins not same."
"I know. The thing is — both were obviously your children, but they each had a different father. It's very rare."
Maude's mouth dropped open. Then she smiled. "If Gabbie okay, might be Clay's little girl, too."
"Might not be too," Wanda warned.
"You help find Gabbie? Find her not dead like Ellie?"
"I'll do what I can," Wanda promised. "Now, I want you to promise something too."
"Will."
"Don't tell anyone else what we have been sharing this evening, Okay?"
"Who believe?"
"Maybe no one, but keep it secret?"
"Secret, like before. You easy to talk to. You come again?"
"I'd like to. And maybe Annie and her friend will come too."
"Be good. I see you out. But have something."
Maude stood and trotted back inside. Wanda followed more slowly and was signing out at reception when Maude returned. "Here. Have these."
Wanda turned and found Maude with a tied up bundle of letters. These were being pressed into her hand. "Read."
"Okay. Then I bring them back."
"Yes."
"Oh, one other thing," Wanda said casually. "When you went to stay with Mickey recently, where were you staying?"

"Nice house. Near park. Was empty."

Wanda had a fleeting vision of the place. "That warm thing, did Mickey keep the box there?"

Maude nodded. "Not all time. Got it from cupboard in train place."

"Did you see him with any papers or flat discs or an envelope?"

"Got something. Big. Yellow. Wrote on it. Posted."

"Did you see what he wrote?" Wanda asked hopefully.

"No. I push trolley. His stuff in it."

"Oh well," Wanda shrugged. "I do have to go. I will come back and see you. And don't worry about the questions. They had to be asked."

Wanda went back to where Fred waited in the car. Once back in the passenger seat, she asked, "How well do you know this area?"

"Well enough, why?"

"Somewhere near River Park there is a rental house..." She gave rough description based on the fleeting image she had seen in Maude's mind.

"Could be a lot of places. They pulled down a lot of old homes and filled the area with smaller ones. What you described – probably that's the north side – across the river."

"Can we drive around? Look see?"

Fred merely grunted and started the car. Wanda rang David to tell him what she was doing and to see if he could find out if any places were for rent, or currently rented. Sometimes, her husband's skill with computers was extraordinary. If this time he was stuck, he could see if Kelso could help.

While driving up and down the streets, Wanda concentrated on the image, and the formless impressions that went with it. Nothing she saw along the street resonated. One thing, she'd had no sense of the river, or crossing it, from Maude. These places too, were way more elaborate than the one Maude recalled.

"Can we look around the park, on the other side of the river?" she suggested to Fred.

"Sure."

"Start close to the park, okay?"

"Can do."

The sense of being close peaked, and Wanda said, "Pull in here," when they were right on the edge of the park. A moment later, David called back.

He began with, "Kelso pulled some strings. He has three addresses near the park that are possibles." He gave her each address and Wanda repeated them aloud. She heard Fred make a noise like a snort, and told David to hold on.

"What," She asked Fred.

"That place opposite is that last address you repeated. Don't know how you guessed it."

"Dav, I think we are at the place. There doesn't seem to be any activity."

His voice came back, "Really? You just got there, and you can tell that from inside a car across the street?"

He knew her too well. He went on. "Wait there. I'll join you and bring your Task Force ID."

"I was just going to look around..."

"Wanda! Do you know who owns that place?"

"Why should I?"

"Exactly. It is owned by Nicholas Gilroy."

"Ah, now isn't that suggestive?" Wanda told him. "Then it is possible the place has been checked over already?"

"How does that follow? Where does Gilroy come into this?"

"Tell you later. Do you think we can get a key?"

"Kelso is working on that."

Wanda settled down to watch, and during the half hour until David arrived, had seen no lights go on, unlike the neighbouring places. She put Maude's letters in the glove box for later.

"How much do reckon the rent on that place would be?" Wanda asked Fred, who gave an estimate.

"If Delaney was staying here, and he was just out of prison, how did he afford it?" Wanda mused. Fred merely grunted.

Finally, a second car drove up, and two people got out. She recognised David immediately, and noticed he was in a suit and tie. His companion, was similarly attired, and when he came over to Fred's car, she recognised him as Detective Kelly.

Wanda emerged so she could talk to them.

"The agent is bringing a key. He will approach the house first. If we are wrong and someone is living there, he will say it is a snap inspection," Kelly told her. "If no one is there, and it looks like the place has been vacated, we will be allowed to go in."

"Will there be someone at the back door in case someone is hiding in there?" Wanda suggested, mostly in jest. If Delaney had been the tenant, no one would be there.

Kelly chuckled, and asked, "What does your intuition tell you?" He glanced at her as he asked it, but Wanda could tell he had positioned himself to watch the house, even as he was trying to make their little group seem like chance met friends, with no interest in any of the houses.

The agent went across to the house and rang the bell, waited and tried again. He then opened the front door and turned on a light. He disappeared inside, but came out almost immediately, and gestured to them.

Wanda entered after Kelly, and immediately looked around.

Someone had been in the house, searching it, for the drawers in the wall units had been hastily shoved back in or left out, chairs turned over, and cushions strewn about, pictures were askew. "Is there a safe in this place?"

The agent answered, "Yes, in the study." He pointed to the relevant opening and Wanda moved that way. She had a glimpse into what would have been a family room, but it had been turned into a flop house with several mattresses on the floor and untidy piles of blankets. David, had followed her, and went in for a closer look.

Finding the safe was easy. The clichéd picture covering had been removed. Wanda pulled on skintight gloves and carefully felt around the edge of the door. She stood and considered. Someone else had started to try to get into the safe, and not with any finesse.

If Gilroy was part of the gang involved with the theft of the power unit, as she privately believed, how had Mickey got to use this house? He must have known he dare not go back to where he had stayed since his release, but did he have the money to rent here? He can't have known who owned it. Or that The Family wanted that unit back. Had they a way of watching him? She looked around for spy-cams but saw nothing suspicious. Delaney and Kemple had got the unit and got away, but there had been others involved. Some had been caught, while running interference for Delaney. Some probably had got away. Had those been here too for a while? Had Delaney or one of the others tried to open the safe?

David come into where she stood. "Can you open it?"

"Yes, but find out if the agent knows the combination."

"What are you thinking?"

"Who else besides Delaney might think he hid something here?"

"Those he was planning to meet and sell it to," David said immediately.

"Okay, and those he stole it from. Would you assume that

person who owns this place would know the combination of the safe here?”

“Maybe. Are you saying the owner would?”

“Uh Huh, and someone that didn't tried to get in.”

“Kelly found the empty box that held the unit – no sign of the specs,” David told her. “So I will see what the agent can tell us.”

The agent, Paul Allen, came in with Kelly following. He went to the safe, and began to turn the knob, standing to hide the numbers he stopped it on. Then he turned the handle to open it. It didn't. He tried the process again with the same result.

“I don't understand,” he admitted. “This is the combination Mr Gilroy gave me.”

David caught Wanda's faint smile, and didn't have to ask what she was thinking. He merely shrugged and suggested, “We can bring in a locksmith in the morning. Has the rest of this place been checked?”

Kelly mentioned, “I think this place has been occupied since we caught Delaney. There is food in the kitchen that is still fresh. I will call for a forensic team to come in, but we should have a closer look everywhere. The searcher may have found what he wanted, or maybe not.”

While everyone else made to go out, Wanda simply said, “I'll look in here.” Then she began to scan the walls and floor as she had when at the scout house. This room had a polished wood floor and scattered mats. It didn't look as if the rabble that had slept in the other room had come in there. However, her first interest was the safe, and she intended to try opening it herself. She had all she needed in a flat waist belt that was hidden by her casual jumper.

Kelly came in just after she had closed the safe again. “Anything?”

“The safe has nothing in it,” she told him quietly.

"Well, checking this place was a worthwhile idea," Kelly admitted. "Still, the forensic guys can go over it. We might pick up prints to identify more of the group. But, right now, David suggests that you disappear out the back and return to the car. The owner has turned up."

"Gilroy?"

Kelly nodded.

As much as she wanted to see the man herself, she knew how David was thinking. If Gilroy was actually one of The Family, she ought to remain out of sight. "Yes. See you."

She crossed the street, aiming for Fred's car, and noticed the expensive late model Mercedes parked in front of him. Assuming that was Gilroy's car, she went behind Fred's blue ford. Only when she was on the nature strip, did she see, Fred lying on the ground. Her danger sense kicked in, as she knelt down to feel for a pulse. Her hand did that as she looked around. Her other hand went into a pocket, and gripped the first thing she felt. One of her less than legal tools. That was all she had time for, before a weighted rope, wrapped around her. She let out the start of a yell, but a firm hand covered her mouth, and she was dragged towards the park.

Her attacker had no way of knowing that she yelled mentally, but he moved fast when he saw David erupt from the house and sprint across the street. She was thrown over his shoulder and he was sprinting away, cutting through to where he had a car, with its boot open.

Wanda was trying to wriggle free the whole time, but the man was strong. He didn't stop her dropping the tool, near Fred's car, and another just as she was tossed into the boot of this other one, and pushed down.

"I will slam this on your arm if you don't move it," she was warned.

She jerked her arm in, but had a grim smile on her face. She recognised the accent of her captor.

David saw the dark figure going into the park and raced in pursuit. Then he felt something hit his legs, tying them together and he fell hard onto the path. When he managed to get his wind back, and untangle the rope, the figure carrying Wanda had gone and he only heard a car revving off.

His whole body had felt the shock of that landing, and as he stumbled back towards the unmarked police car, he didn't realise how his face looked. It took him a while to realise that he had been gone long enough for an ambulance and two marked police cars to arrive.

"David!" Kelso called when he saw David under the streetlight. "What happened to you?"

"Someone took Wanda," he was intending to say, but the voice that came out was garbled.

"Here," Kelso called, and one of the paramedics came over.

"I'm okay," David tried to say, but he was pushed into a sitting position at the back of the ambulance.

"You have blood all over your face, possibly a broken nose," Kelso told him. "Let them look at you."

David tried to stand, but he was pushed back as the paramedic checked, asking if various things hurt. Finally, they began to gently wash the blood from his face, saying most of it was from the blood nose. Then they held up two fingers and asked how many he could see.

"Two," he tried to say.

The paramedic suggested, "Hold up the same number of yours."

It was proof he was speaking gibberish. He did, as told, holding up two, only to hear, "I only held up one. I will be taking you in to the hospital to get that head of yours x-rayed."

David tried to struggle then, but Kelly spoke up. "Is this Wanda's?"

David nodded cautiously.

"Do you think she dropped it on purpose?" he persisted.

Thinking on it, he thought she probably had, so he nodded.

"Okay." Kelly gestured to one of the uniformed men, and asked them to follow the path and see if they found anything else that might have been dropped. He turned his attention back to David. "Go and get checked over. This routine stuff can be done by us, do you agree?"

David reluctantly nodded again. His head was beginning to ache like a drum being pounded. Considering his symptoms, he realised he may have knocked himself out for a few minutes, and may even have concussion. In fact, he was even having trouble worrying about Wanda.

***

Martin stopped in his doorway when he saw Kelly coming up the path. The policeman beckoned him out, so he locked up and approached.

"What now?" he growled. "Won't I ever be left alone?"

"Not while you are such a helpful resource," Kelly remarked. "I believe you walk to school with Annie Jamieson."

"Well yeah. What do you want her for?"

"David suggested that she might be able to help with something."

"I usually meet her at the corner. What's up?"

"Wanda is missing. She dropped something, and David hopes she might have impressed something on it that Annie might sense."

"She might, but shouldn't you ask her folks?"

"Do they know what she can do?" Kelly asked.

Martin shook his head. "And I don't think she really wants people to know about it."

"I understand. I don't think David would have suggested it, except, we are worried about Wanda."

"She strikes me as very capable," Martin suggested. "Why didn't David come himself?"

"He won't be let out of hospital until later. We found where Delaney had been staying, and went to search the place. Someone had been there before us, and likely was disturbed. We believe they wanted to know if the police found anything."

Annie recognised Kelly, and trotted closer. "Why are you here?"

Kelly explained, and Annie felt herself tremble. "If I can help, of course. Where did she go missing?"

When Kelly gave more detail, Martin said, "I know where that is."

Kelly brought out a plastic bag, and passed it to Annie. She didn't ask what the slender metal tool was, but Martin gave a low whistle. He watched as Annie took it out, and saw her go even paler than she had.

"What's the matter?" Martin asked quietly.

"There was someone on the ground, an oldish man. Whoever had this was looking around, but something dropped down on her, so she couldn't get free, and a hand covered her mouth."

Kelly was staring at her, amazed. "That is pretty well what happened. Whoever attacked her took off with her to a car. Try this one."

Kelly took the first tool back and replaced it in the plastic bag. He took a second from a different pocket.

Annie, was less hesitant this time. She had the definite feeling that Wanda had somehow hoped she would have this chance. She had to concentrate harder. Telling her mind her hands were completely uncovered.

"There's a car with its boot up, and Wanda is trying to get free, but...I think it's for show. I don't feel fear, or terror. Does that help at all?"

"It might when I get David's opinion. Could you tell what sort of car it was?"

"No. It was dark, mostly. I just get impressions. Look, please don't tell anyone what I can do, okay?"

"I understand, and no I don't think I will need to. Thank you."

"Oh, Martin," Kelly recalled his other reason for coming. "Can the police have permission to look through your garage again?"

"What for now?"

"To see if your father, or the others left an envelope here with important data in. We weren't aware it was missing when we searched the first time."

"Do you need to check the house too?"

"You removed all your father's stuff to the garage didn't you?"

"Pretty sure. What was the envelope like?"

"I am told A4 sized. One of the strong yellow type."

"I didn't see anything like that in the house," Martin said thoughtfully. "If need be, you can look again, but we have to get going to school now."

"Has your father been back?"

"I warned him to stay away," Martin said. "Told the bastard about the restraining order too. I don't think he wants to go back into jail. I said he had to contact you guys if he wanted any of his stuff."

Kelly chuckled. "I will suggest we re-check there as soon as possible. Do you have the key for the new lock we put on it?"

"Yes, hang on. I keep it on me."

Martin retrieved a key chain from his pocket, and took one key off the ring. "The spare is inside, but I don't think Kemple will likely find it."

"Thanks," Kelly said. "If you like, I can take you part way to school."

"Please don't," Martin said with a groan. "I am trying to improve my reputation. What you could do is tell me if you find anything important."

Any idea of getting away when the boot opened was quashed by the presence of the man with the gun, standing just to the side of the big man who reached in to get her.

"I can get myself out," Wanda told him. "So hands off!"

It didn't work. She was allowed to climb out, and look around, but that was all. She was grabbed and pulled out of the garage and into the house along a short passage. Leo Tatarovich, her captor, had not recognised her. The reverse was not true – now in the well-lit passage, Wanda was certain. What she wasn't certain of, was if this was the house where Nicholas Gilroy lived. As they moved into the living area, she decided it wasn't. More likely, it was where her uncles, Leo and Stephan lived. The house did not seem to have any feminine touches.

In the living room, the furniture was second hand, armchairs and a couch that didn't match. Wanda was shoved into one of the chairs, and whilst the gun holder thought he had her scared, Leo dragged her arms back behind her and tied them.

So far they hadn't given any indication of what they wanted from her, but she could guess with fair accuracy. Nor did they talk once she was restrained. That caused her think that they were obeying orders, and had none past this point – yet. She watched the man with the gun, trying to get an impression from him. It was likely this man was also a member of The Family, but there was no likeness to any of them she had met previously. Leo paced restlessly. Maybe he was expecting to be reprimanded – did that mean that one of the "Fathers" would be coming? She only feared meeting one of them, Theo. But Theo should still be in Austria. She didn't see him wanting to give up his power base there.

"So, what's the deal here?" Wanda said. "Now that you have the one you think is the weakest member of the Atlas Task Force."

They didn't react. Well, she had patience to spare, and the respite gave her the chance to think back over the events at the rental house. She had missed something, she guessed. There had been a security system in the house, but it had shown all green and off on the control pad inside the door. She had seen the sensors in the room with the safe, going red when she moved. Had there been sensors that didn't betray themselves? Possible....maybe the men had been told to stay out of that room, and there was a way of keeping sure they did. But why?

Her private guess about Gilroy's involvement, had been proved, to her own satisfaction. When he had heard the house was being visited by police, he had gone there himself. To distract the police? To find out if they had learnt anything? Did he think they might? Had Leo been inside checking things when the police had arrived? Had he warned Gilroy, or had that been the call from the agent?

Lots of questions went through Wanda's mind as she stared at both men. The one that stuck most was – had they found the specs she was searching for? No, if they had, they would not have wanted someone to question. They would be better off asking Delaney, except he was in the remand centre still. Had the message Delaney sent, been about the specs as she believed? Is that how they found out that Delaney had been trying to get a bigger share of the action?

Then she recalled what Maude had said, about getting the box from a train station, a big busy one. She should have told Fred about that, or David. The question of where Delaney had sent the specs before going to meet the buyer's intermediary, now had major importance. Had he sent that to the contact or the buyer direct? It would be bad if he had been caught doing the delivery but the buyers had already got the specs. They had spooked and left, but might still be able to contact Mickey if they hadn't.

By the time Gilroy arrived, both of her captors were fidgeting uneasily. They were sensing that their captive was not frightened of them. In her first glimpse of the man, she did a swift comparison between him and Leo. There was a likeness, but Gilmore was slender, more like Stephan who was shadowing him into the room.

"Well, well, well, I finally get to meet Uncle Nicky."

Gilroy went rigid. Stephan moved to get a better view. Leo went red in the face and growled, "You!"

"It's great to see you again, Uncle Leo. Obviously you managed to stay free after I helped you out of that Austrian lock up."

There it was. Wanda kept her amusement strictly internal. Leo and Stephan owed her. It wasn't her fault they had soon been captured again, not really.

Now Gilroy, formerly Nicholai Tatarovitch, knew she wasn't just an interfering police agent, but 'Family'. He had to change his planned approach. He wasn't to know that she would prefer to deny the relationship and usually did.

If they thought she wouldn't understand the rapid exchange in Russian, they were wrong. Leo came and grabbed the Task Force ID, and yanked it from around her neck.

"How did a useless piece of trash get to be involved with police? Are you one of them?"

"Are you serious? The arrogant piece of crud that sired you had me totally fixed in jail. No police force in the world would let me join up. How is Grand-daddy anyway?" She knew he was dead, but wasn't going to admit it.

"He's dead," Gilroy said flatly. "I'm sure you knew that."

"Nah! Last I saw of that piece of crud, he was trying to strangle me. Next thing I know I am being dragged out of the river. At least I had managed to help your sister! Which is more than any of you did."

"Your mother!" Leo growled. "I don't know how she managed to manage to birth a useless piece of trash like you."

"Not so useless! I helped you to escape."

"Enough!" Gilroy said, just loud enough to be heard. Leo subsided, and that told Wanda who was in charge here. "I, for one, am glad that your mother –"

"Your sister," Wanda emphasised.

"...Got free of him," Gilroy finished, giving her a glare for interrupting. "However, I still want to know how you got to be tied up with the police."

"Actually, not the police. The taskforce is a mixture of agencies. As for me, well, I'm their security expert."

Wanda smirked, and Stephan actually smiled at the irony. "And before you think I am lying, just remember some purple diamonds."

She was amused to see all three of her uncles shudder.

"Cursed things," Gilroy snapped. "Even you didn't escape the effect."

"Perhaps," Wanda considered. "But I think they really twisted the mind of your sire, and good riddance to him. Anyway, as I was about to say earlier, Ivana is back with her husband and daughter."

"What?" Leo roared. "Father said you were –"

"He was wrong! You three didn't have just one sister, you had three!"

"No…" Stephan said, his voice shaking.

"What are you talking about?" Gilroy demanded.

"Anneleise, the woman he pretended to marry so that he could usurp her inheritance, had triplets."

Wanda was pleased by the effect of her bombshell. "Likely that bastard didn't stick around long enough to even know she was pregnant. He must have been shocked when Ivana was brought to his family."

Gilroy moved to the other chair and slumped into it. His mind was conflicted, having been taught that the women of the family were to be protected. He had not been able to help the sister he had known of. Now he was wondering about the two sisters he had not known about.

"You don't have to believe me, but if I could find out, you can. My mother was Katya Antov, nee Tatarovich. She's dead now."

It was Leo who finally got back to the intended questions. "Family or no, you still work for the police."

"So? They are paying for the best available security expert. Rather amusing, I know. Anyway, just to shut you up, I did get the safe open in that house and it was as empty as it was when it was installed."

They had other questions, but Wanda fended off most by claiming that she had been there to help find something and that was all. She wasn't privy to the details of what the task force was doing.

"You'd be better off asking your flunkey, Delaney."

The four men, which included the one who had been with Leo, and who was saying nothing, were all but yelling their thoughts. They intended to talk to Delaney, and had devised a way to get him out. The plan though was not being thought in detail. All that was clear was that they knew him, but he had interfered with their business.

The fourth man, the one she didn't know, asked, "Whose side are you on then?"

"My own!" Wanda snapped. "Unless you can convince me that I am better off with relatives. My unlamented grandfather soured me. I don't hold a grudge against my uncles, and who are you anyway?"

"We don't like traitors," the same man told her.

"How can I be a traitor when I only learnt about you all shortly before my grandfather tried to kill me?"

"You know now."

"Yeah, I do," Wanda agreed belligerently. "And I answered your damn questions. If you wanted more information you'd have done better to have snagged my minder. However, since you haven't I have a request. You get Delaney here and once he's answered your questions, let me at him."

"Why?" Gilroy asked, coming out of his shock.

"Why?" Wanda echoed. "Because I don't like bullies. I want to get even with him for the way he set up his wife, and if I can, to find out if he was telling the truth when he told her that one of her baby girls, who he had taken from her, is really still alive."

"What can you do to him?" Gilroy demanded.

"That's my secret. So, if he won't tell you the truth ...let me at him."

"No," Gilroy decided.

"Don't be so hasty, Nik," the fourth man suggested. "Delaney is scum, no better than his useless mate – your ex-brother-in-law. I think I want to see what your niece can do to him."

He had seen the expression Wanda hadn't tried to hide.

"I still don't..." Gilroy began to say as he tried to see right into her.

Stephan blurted, "She did something to father so he spilled

all he knew to the police. He didn't try to have us blamed instead."

Wanda wanted to pump her fist and yell, "Yes!" Stephan at least was as good as an ally.

Gilroy gestured to Leo. "Cut her loose. She can use that spare third guest room."

"What about those step-brats of yours?" Leo demanded.

"I'll talk to them," Gilroy promised. "And you..."he looked at Wanda, "You'll do as we ask?"

"Depends. I don't use guns, or kill people, but if its locks you want opened, and your brother experts can't manage, then I'm in."

Without warning, Leo lashed out with his fist, punching her on the left ear. "You'd better learn fast that our women do as they are told, and if they don't, they are punished."

Wanda's head was pushed so hard that her neck hurt. Obviously, she had gone too far with Leo.

"Fine! Now I know," she muttered, as she felt her wrists freed.

Leo grabbed the back of her jumper and hauled her up. "You leave, you're finished," he warned.

"Wouldn't dream of it," she said sarcastically.

Wanda retreated to the bedroom Stephan pointed to, and collapsed onto the bed. She hoped she hadn't looked as tottery as she felt. Once she no longer felt like she was about to fall over, she gently massaged the painful side of her head, and made sure her ear hadn't been squashed. After half an hour of using some mind tricks she knew, she felt the pain recede and decided she was functional.

She took amusement from the fact that her uncles hadn't even searched her, so that she still had most of her tools and her phone and stuff they'd never thought to look for. Then she realised that she ought to text David before they realised their mistake. She texted as words, the first meaning she was okay, then one implying 'with the enemy'. Normally, an answer would come promptly, but five minutes passed, and she realised she was tensing up. What could have happened to David? She tried to send him a thought, but the effort started her head pounding. She had just thought of calling Kelso, when her door opened.

The man she didn't know paused there until she gestured him in. "Are you another relative?"

"More distant, yes. I use the name Eduardo."

"Hi then, Eduardo. Did they tell you my name?"

"Wanda, yes. Can I ask you some things?"

He was being polite, not demanding so Wanda said, "I guess so."

"What was your interest in Kemple?"

"Him? Personally, none. I was sent to follow him from that station in town. To see what he did. Make work."

Wanda decided that telling him, minus some details, wouldn't hurt.

"Ah, yes. Nik's stepsons passed on a message sent through their cousin." He went on to ask, "Will they be looking for you?"

"Probably. Didn't my minder high tail it after me?"

"We blocked him."

"Ah, right. Well, I guess that gives me a bit of freedom."

"Why do you really want Delaney?"

She sensed no antagonistic thoughts from him, and she mentioned several things she believed of Mickey.

"The police only trust me so far, they reckon I have no scruples, but he enjoys hurting kids and framing others for it."

"I understand," Eduardo said quickly. "It is why I insisted my sister should leave Kemple. How well do you know Kemple's son?"

Wanda sensed the abrupt subject change was to trick her, but the ploy wouldn't work on her.

"I have been cultivating him and a girl, because they have a soft spot for Mickey's wife."

If Eduardo was checking her out, he didn't realise he was giving himself away to her. She decided, cautiously, that he was more like Stephan.

"How's your head?"

"Almost back to normal," Wanda lied. "Is that Uncle Leo's usual greeting to a family member?"

"It is to those who irritate him."

"Well, I'm in trouble then. I irritate people on a regular basis."

"I'd noticed. But, you are welcome to stay. Help yourself to food from the fridge if you are hungry"

"Thanks. When might you get Delaney?"

"Tomorrow.

Wanda just grinned.

The big man who slipped into the seat opposite caused Kevin Kemple to want to dart out and run. However, a furtive glance towards the exit showed him two more men, casually placed to prevent him leaving.

"So, Kemple, what's so important that you came close enough for a second lesson," Leo Tatarovich spoke softly, with his face leaning over to be within six inches of Kemple's lip quivering, pale face.

Fearing another beating, Kemple quickly stammered, "Delaney sent me a message. I had to tell your boss that he has something equally as valuable as the original merchandise."

"What?" Leo demanded.

"All he said was, 'I have the paperwork', whatever that means." Kemple trembled, seeing the big man's eyes seeming to bore right into him.

"Did you see this mythical paperwork?"

"No, but Mickey said it had been with the heavy package. He had all that when we split. He was going back to where he was dossing and I headed back home."

Leo sat back and made a slight hand gesture. One of the other men moved closer so Leo could whisper directions into his ear. The man moved off again, while taking out his mobile phone.

"So where did Mickey hide this paperwork?" Leo was leaning back, seemingly the comment was a casual one.

"He didn't say. He just said it was safe. No one would find it." Kemple hoped they'd believe him, because Delaney had told him to get the envelope with it in, from where it was hidden.

"So, what use is it to us?" Leo challenged.

"Mickey says, it's as good as the having the heavy part and if you can get him out, he'll take you to it, and then you can let him go."

"That's not for me to decide," Leo announced. "I'd be inclined to want to drop him from the back of a fast moving semi on a busy freeway. That's what people who try to double cross us deserve."

Kemple's voice had risen in pitch when he said, "I didn't know Mickey was doing that."

"No, of course not," Leo sneered. "But let's say I believe you. So all the message was, 'Get me out and I will give you this paperwork'?"

Kemple nodded.

"How did your friend make a deal with our contacts?" Leo demanded.

"I don't know anything about it," Kemple squealed, as Leo's fist gripped the front of his shirt.

Leo released him, but continued to glare while he waited for the answer from the man with the phone.

"Where will you be tonight? Your house?"

"No, my bastard of a son has kicked me out. I thought I'd find a woman to doss with."

The man who had made the call came back and whispered in Leo's ear.

"Okay, Kemple. Your message was delivered. You stay around. When we have the stuff from Mickey, there will be a little reward for you. Five hundred dollars. Ring this number and we'll see you get it."

"F...Five hundred," Kemple stammered, taking a card from Leo's hand. "O...Okay."

"Have another coffee on us," Leo said as he stood up. He drew some change from his pocket and put it on the table. "Enjoy it for a while, you understand?"

Kemple nodded and his gut began to relax after the men left the café. Then his mind went into an argument with itself. Greed, and need, for the promised reward vied with the idea of getting far, far, away. Greed won, since it went with the idea of, 'stay around, or we will find you and bash you again.'

The same fear of the big man, prompted Kemple to leave via the alley door. He had a job to do for Mickey and he didn't want anyone to know about it. Even though Mickey had been kept in a more secure section of the remand prison, word could be passed. He had been told, "Empty your box and keep it safe."

Then, when he had been bailed out, the bail agent had given him a letter from Mickey. That had been the message for Gilroy. He was relieved that part was over. All he had to do now was take a large letter from his post office box and put it in a locker at Southern Cross Station. It was as well that he hadn't wanted to use his garage again. He would be sent back into remand if he broke that damned restraining order. He'd get even with his brat, for that.

First though, he'd better see which one of his three regular women would let him spend the night. Tomorrow, he'd move somewhere else. Mickey had mentioned a name, Long Lonny. He had rooms for people lying low.

It wasn't until he was back with Southern Sal, and had watched the street from her window for half an hour, that he felt sure he had eluded any potential watchers. Then he sent Sal out for a feast of chicken and salad, and while she was out, found a place to stash the locker key, and some tape to hold it in place. He'd retrieve it before he left.

Feeling more in control after a pleasant night with Sal, he considered staying longer. Perhaps even marrying her. He needed a new place while he fixed his bastard of a son.

The police should have locked him up! He should have been thoroughly discredited, especially after that drug business last year. Instead, he had come home, the house had been searched.

Kemple restrained himself from snarling. He'd only just had time to text Mickey a warning to remove the merchandise from the garage. No, he'd better go to Lonny's place, when he left next day.

The phone call came in the afternoon, after he had settled into one of Lonny's cellars. Mickey sounded pissed, or maybe he'd discovered that the guys he was trying to fleece didn't play nice.

"You done it?" Mickey demanded.

"Yes, I have the key."

"No one was watching you?"

"No, I was very careful."

"Stay there. I'll come get the key. I've got one more bit of business after this and I'll be heading north."

"You're not giving those bastards what they want?" Kemple asked, seeing his 500 dollars vanishing into thin air.

"What does it matter to you? They know you don't have it, or know where it is. Them foreign bastards can whistle for it. Their contacts still want it and if I get it to them, I'll get the money. One hundred thousand dollars. I can use that money more than they can, and a quarter of that is yours if you don't cave in."

"What if they find you again?" The idea of twenty five thousand dollars was like a glittering present, and glee bubbled up inside him at the thought that his wife's relatives would be done out of it.

"They won't. I got myself looking like someone else – old Spider Scarface. He likes the idea of being impersonated, then he has an alibi. Anyway, I'll be there tonight."

Kemple grinned in anticipation – twenty five thousand dollars!

Late in the evening, Mickey slipped into the room occupied by Kemple. The signs of the bashing he had been given were still vivid on his face, but his left cheek had been painted to look like a scald scar, and looked covered in a mesh of black lines.

"You okay, mate?" Kemple asked in alarm. Twinges from his

own bad experience sent pain along his arms and legs.

"They didn't dare get too rough. They wanted that envelope. Took them to the locker I did have it in, and while they were going through the junk I left there, I got away. What number did you get?"

Kemple felt for his keys, and found the locker key. "41" he said and Mickey roared with laughter.

"Do you mean to tell me, that while they were cursing about not finding it, the effing envelope was only 2 lockers away?"

Kemple joined the laughter. "So when you meeting the buyer?"

"Saturday," Mickey told him.

"What about your other business, Mickey?"

"I'm owed payment for some major favours I did before I got put inside. I can't stay around waiting for that investment to mature, so we agreed on a figure."

"Oh, yes?" Kemple was interested.

"Thought the guy was thinking of welching, so I set the ruskies on him. I reckon I have him so worried now that he'll pay up faster. Tried to convince me he needed time, but I know he always keeps money stashes around...for emergencies. Anyway, he reckons he has to maintain a perfectly spotless reputation, but he knows that I know a lot of his dirty secrets.

Later that evening, Lonny brought a cordless phone into the room and handed it to Mickey.

"What is it?" he demanded of the caller. He listened and then blurted, "You know I wasn't there!" A pause, then, "You'd better not try welching on me, mate! I'll give you two days."

After shoving the phone back at Lonny, Mickey began to pace.

"I reckon the cops are onto my mate," he growled.

"What for," Kemple prompted.

"Dunno for sure. He's got two whackos claiming he's their Pa. Might well be, for all the interest he has in sharing his money. Only reason he puts up with that girl of his, is that she's worth money."

Episode 13

Clues Come Together

Chapter 1

David was fit to be tied by the time morning came. He was out of his mind, worrying about his wife. He'd already called Kelso twice, hoping for news. What he had been told was still worrying him.

If he could look at things calmly, and without the still throbbing head, he would have realised two things. First, he didn't feel she was in bad trouble and his sister-in-law hadn't rung him. Second, he would have remembered to check his message relay – a precaution he and Wanda had set up for when they didn't want to seem associated.

When the morning's dose of strong pain killer kicked in, he finally thought of it. He retrieved the text message and had to decipher the mixture of agreed code words and impromptu ones. In one way, the more he read, the better he felt. She was safe, had met three uncles, they had plans to get at Delaney to question him, and she'd have her chance too.

He rang Kelso, and gave him what he had. The retired policeman was alarmed by the assumption that The Family would spring Delaney from remand and was going to warn the police. It meant though, that the people who had stolen the power unit did not have the specs, and Wanda was in a position to find out if Delaney told them anything.

Even knowing that, David couldn't settle. There were things

he needed to do. He had to trust that Wanda wasn't out of her depth, and resist the urge to rush out and find her. What he had intended to be doing was keep an eye on Jeremy Carson and see if he reacted to the carefully worded articles that were to be inserted into that morning's newspapers. There were two well separated, seemingly unrelated articles.

He'd snagged a paper from the morning tea trolley, and had it open so the two articles were showing.

"Good Morning, Mr Davis," a different voice greeted him.

David stopped pacing and spun around. This wasn't the nurse who had taken over his care, but he recognised her at once.

"Hello, Mrs Jamieson," he answered in surprise.

"How are you feeling?"

He grinned in spite of himself. "Like I went face-to-face with a footpath. When can I expect the doctor?"

"When he gets here to do his rounds. I was surprised to find you here."

"Yeah," David said, feeling sheepish. "It wasn't planned, and it is nice to see a friendly face."

"Good. So sit down while I do your obs."

He obeyed, but wondered at the frown that appeared on Marilyn Jamieson's face. He waited to see if she broached the reason.

"You're still interested in Maude Hartley," she remarked as she moved the open paper. "Do the police expect to gain anything from those articles?"

"Yes and no," David summarised. "We did hear that Delaney told Maude that one of her girls was alive, and implied he knew where. Maybe someone else knows something."

His nurse continued her tasks automatically before saying more.

"I'm not happy Annie is involved, from what I have heard of Maude's husband, but she is. She asked me about adoptions, back when all that business with Maude happened. I told her, that in those days, women without husbands were often forced to give up their babies for adoption. The details of mother and adopted parents were sealed so neither party knew who the other was."

David asked quietly, "Did that happen to you?" His answer was a faint nod. He went on, "Kelso, the former policeman I am working with, mentioned something about that, but he is hoping to be allowed access to those records."

He felt the hand taking his pulse tense, and went on, "He has doubts of success though. We might have to resort to contacting some of the on-line find your parent or child groups."

"They may help," Marilyn agreed. "But there was one other thing I recalled when I read about them finding one of Maude's girls."

"Oh? What was that?" David was suddenly intent on hearing what she would say.

"About 10-15 years ago, there was a scandal where police uncovered an illegal adoption service. Apparently, some of the children that passed through that service had been abducted, specifically because they possessed certain looks."

"Like someone wanted a child that looked like them?"

Marilyn nodded. "Some of the children being cared for had been bought from unwed mothers, mostly as new-borns, though some were older. The older ones were harder to place, though. When the premises were raided, some of the older ones were in a dreadful state. A couple died, soon after they were placed in foster care by the authorities."

"Where did this take place?" David asked.

"They kept the children somewhere in the country, but the group had offices in Melbourne."

"So after the raid, what happened?" David prompted.

"The Department of Human Services took the children, placed the older ones in foster homes. They found the records of the group, but they were no help. The names didn't tally with any missing children, and the supposed mothers could not be found. Of course, the real mothers didn't dare come forward."

"Thank you for telling me this," David said, sincerely, even while realising that Annie's mother had secrets. "I think I know where Annie gets her caring heart."

"How will you know if you find Maude's girl? DNA?"

"Yes. Maude kept hair from both the girls, but even without that, they can tell if a particular person is likely related. In this sad case, having the hair made it definite."

Marilyn Jamieson abruptly dropped the subject. "Now, you jarred your whole body, really hard. So you should take it easy for a few days. You will probably feel stiff for a while too. Gentle exercise, and don't overdo the stretches."

"Yes, Mam," David grinned. "Say hi to Annie for me."

"I will. Can I assure her that your partner is alright?"

"How...did you get to think she wasn't?"

"Annie rang me. She said Martin had heard something, and could I listen out for news."

"Wanda, I believe, is right where she wanted to be, and whilst she had been forbidden a certain course of action, I believe she is now in a position to do it."

"Oh, dear! That is a lot of words to say very little."

"I can't discuss some things, but Wanda can generally talk herself out of trouble. I have had a brief text message from her, so I know she is okay if little else."

"Well, I hope you are right. Now, rest!"

As soon as he was alone, David rang Kelso again and related what Mrs Jamieson had recalled. It was an unexpected response to the articles. Kelso promised to have someone check for the records of such an investigation. David wondered if the people involved were still around and could be found. Maybe they would be willing to talk? If they did not fear retaliation from any of their past clients.

Chapter 2

David found himself wanting to doze off and decided he needed to get out of the car and move around. First though, he checked the rear vision mirror and made sure there was no activity at Jeremy Carson's house. Since he had taken over from another of Kelso's men three hours ago, Carson had made two trips somewhere and the housekeeper had made another. He wasn't expected to follow Carson and find out what he was doing, he was to watch out for Mickey Delaney.

If he was challenged by any authority, he had his ID and would imply he was watching for the two who were supposedly stalking Carson. A nice, sedentary task to keep his mind away from worrying about his wife, and because he was meant to be resting. And he sure couldn't blend into a crowd with his nose being held together by brilliant white plaster tape.

"What the hell happened to you?"

David spun around too quickly and felt light headed. "Oh, hello Martin. I wasn't expecting to see you."

He reached out to the old tree near him on the nature strip to steady himself.

"I'm on my way to work. I come this way sometimes. Are you watching Carson?"

David leant against the tree and gave his cover story.

"Should you even be out of bed?" Martin asked with concern.

"I, ah, missed that bit of the discharge instructions." David forced a grin. "It was only a trip. I landed on my face."

"Do I want to know how come?"

"I think your question really is – do you dare ask me how come?"

"Yeah," Martin agreed.

"We were checking out a house where Mickey Delaney had been staying before his arrest. A place owned, as it happens, by your cousins' step-father."

145

Martin made a soundless, "Oh," then asked, "Does that mean you now think he's into something crooked?"

"It's suggestive, but not proof of anything."

"But?"

"But Gilroy used to have another name and he and his two brothers are relatives of my wife."

"Is that why she is staying at one of his houses?" Martin blurted. "She said she didn't want them to know she was around."

"That would have been smart," David admitted, "and was her intention. However one of them must have been hanging around the house when we arrived."

"You and Wanda?"

"No, not just us. He must have seen Wanda duck out when Gilroy arrived and decided to grab her. And, since she let him, she obviously decided it was a good time for a reunion."

"Do you always talk in riddles?" Martin asked. "So you knew where she went?"

"She sent a message to let me know she was okay, but couldn't give me a location. Do you know where the house is?"

"It's at 56 Evans Street. My cousins are staying there too, since their step-father is annoyed with them. They saw Wanda this morning at breakfast and told me my 'friend' was actually a cop trying to get evidence against me. I told them that she was more likely checking them out. That shouldn't have shut them up, but it did. I think, they were told not to mention her."

David laughed. "Your cousins are such innocents."

"I'd call them idiots," Martin contested. "But if Wanda is related to their step-father – does that mean I'm related to her in some way?"

"It would be very distant. He's from a European branch of the family," David revealed. "Hadn't you better be getting to work?"

"Yeah. I've got Friday off school. A teacher training day or something. If I can help, let me know."

"I'll keep the offer in mind," David agreed. "But please, don't try anything on your own."

"From anyone else, that would be a challenge, but no, I won't. I know there is more going on than you can tell me."

"Thanks, mate!" David smiled, using the Australian terminology. "Oh, has Abbie Carson been at school since Tuesday?"

"Nope. Hasn't been all week. Annie has been sending notes to her, but hasn't had any reply. Is she in trouble again?"

"I don't think so. I was just curious."

Martin headed off and David watched for a while before getting back into the rented car. He took the portable radio from the passenger seat and called Kelso. His conversation mentioned no names, and relayed the gist of the information. Only the address in Evans Street was given openly. The risk that the people of interest were listening on that frequency was low. Kelso said he'd put someone to watch that place, since the people were interested in Delaney.

David added, "I've had nothing from Wanda to say he's there."

Less than half an hour later, his certainty was completely upset. He felt, as he sometimes did, the effect of his wife's mood – she was seething. Moments later, his phone pinged an incoming message.

"B's KO'd me! D is here! More L8r."

David reported this immediately to Kelso, along with a request not to interfere yet. At the same time he had mental fingers crossed that his wife knew what she was doing and would have the time to do it.

Wanda had woken, immediately aware of the lingering effect of the sedative drug that she hadn't been aware of getting. She was dreading the secondary effect she was likely to have. She got up at once from the bed, where she had collapsed, or been put. She hadn't been locked in, so they must have knocked her out as a precaution against something. Eating something would probably be a good thing, but first she went out to the back yard and sat on the grass. There were loose clippings everywhere, since the lawn had been cut by some handyman earlier that afternoon.

Her watch told her it was nearly five, but as she hadn't sensed anyone in the house, she guessed the cousins had been told to stay away, and the others expected her to still be out cold. Bully for them, more so if the after-reaction set in. She had to try something, so she could function in a controlled fashion.

A listener might have thought her mad, talking to herself, but she wasn't. She knew, that sometimes, some invisible power worked with her. The pious might say it was God, but Wanda felt this was an even older power. Right now, she really needed to be in control, so she thought how she needed to overcome the chemicals in her system, to be able to get answers from a very evil man who killed little children and used women to hide behind.

The faintest of breezes caressed her face. She felt her mind clear, and a feeling of confidence grew.

"Thank you," she thought strongly. When she stood to return to the house, she realised the feeling of dizziness had gone too.

With no one around, she did a quick scouting foray of the house, checking the house phone and finding it working, memorised the number without particular intent. It was just the way her memory was. Anything she saw, she remembered.

Wanda was helping herself to a late lunch when she heard sounds from the door that opened into the garage. She didn't need to see what was happening, because the senses of rage, pain and disgust – along with some truly vile language, warned her that her uncles were back with Delaney.

Chapter 3

Wanda ignored her uncles as they wrestled the shorter form of Delaney through to a room off the passage. He didn't notice her, since he was still trying his hardest to get free. She didn't bother trying to figure out how they had sprung him, her uncle Nicholai likely hacked the justice department computers. She knew he was capable of that. It was obvious that they had already tried to get information from Mickey, somewhere, and if they were bringing him here, must have failed. That wasn't surprising. Delaney boasted that he could keep secrets.

Stephan came into the kitchen. "Leo wants you." He jerked his head in the direction Mickey had been taken.

Eduardo met them outside a door. "You reckon you can make that Neanderthal talk?"

"Let me at him," Wanda met the implied challenge. "You must have been too easy on him. He was still fighting."

They heard banging from behind a partly opened door. Eduardo stalked back in, followed by Stephan. Wanda paused briefly to put her phone into silent mode, and text David a terse heads up before strutting in and giving the scene one sweeping glance.

Delaney was being restrained by Leo, who had him in a painful hammerlock.

In a whisper, she asked Stephan, "What exactly do you want to know?"

"The specs that came with the prototype. They weren't with it," he told her.

"What would they be in?" Wanda pretended not to know.

"An envelope for the wad of printouts, and a mini cd with the activation program." That was Leo answering, so Wanda looked his way.

"Would you recognise the stuff if you saw it?"

He nodded deliberately, but his furious eyes warned her that she had better not try to double cross him. She simply stared back, eyes shuttered, and betraying nothing. She shrugged to indicate that Leo should release his prisoner. He glared at Stephan and Eduardo, who retreated with every sign of relief. Leo, it seemed, intended to stay and watch, perhaps hoping Mickey would beat her to a pulp. He didn't matter if he didn't interfere. When the door clicked shut, Leo gave Mickey a powerful shove that sent him sprawling on the floor, which, Wanda felt was more solid than wood. Probably concrete. He sprung up, eyes on the door. Leo seemed unconcerned, and she guessed the door, and probably the walls too, were solid.

Delaney turned, caught sight of Wanda. "Well, who are you? A plaything for me?"

Leo was smirking as Delaney slowly neared her. Wanda however, casually brushed imaginary dust from one sleeve, and said quite clearly, "No, I am your worst nightmare."

She began to move towards his left side, and then to circle him, as he began to turn to keep her in his sight. Delaney laughed and leered but seemed unaware of what he was doing. "Oh, no, girlie, you're just what I need right now. It don't mean this little present will make me talk."

"You'd like to think so," Wanda told him in a flat voice. "And, no, the ruskie won't interfere, even if you begged him for help."

In a low voice, that forced Delaney to concentrate to hear her, she began talking dirty, implying promises of what he could do if he told the ruskies what they wanted to know. It was affecting him, it was obvious. His mind was drifting from defiance to lust, and Wanda hoped this would lower his barriers and put him into the suggestive hypnotic state she was trying for. Yet, if the severe beating he had already been subjected to hadn't broken him, he might be too dense for her initial plan to work.

"Nah, I don't need no help to take you. What did you do for

them to hate you so much?" Delaney added an oblique warning.

Wanda didn't answer that, just changed her low voiced words to something else, and Delaney stopped talking again to listen, and when she stopped circling, he kept turning. She had him.

"Mickey, come here and look at me."

"I knew you'd want me, girlie," he said, the leer must have been instinctive. He stopped approaching at a gesture from Wanda.

"Yes, Mickey. I want you to tell me the answer to every question I ask you."

He stood waiting, still leering.

"Did you take a metallic box from a truck?"

"Yes."

"What was in it?"

"Something worth mega bucks."

"Did you know it was there?"

"No."

"What did you do about it, Mickey?"

"I had a real good offer."

"Who from. What was his name?"

"Lochek."

"Where did you keep the box until you were to see him?"

"In the garage."

"What garage?"

"At the house..."

Wanda heard Leo utter a curse. She hoped David was hearing the conversation and could pass the information to Kelso. When she left, they hadn't thought to look there. Yet, she had the feeling that even under hypnosis, Delaney had to lie.

"What was the address of the house?"

Delaney mentioned the street where he had been staying, but the image in his mind wasn't that one. It was like Kemple's place. Should she probe further? He'd had to flee from there.

"Was the box there from the time you got it to the day you

went to deliver it?"

"Yeah."

"No it wasn't" Leo snarled.

"Where did you take the box, Mickey, after you left the first house?"

She didn't think he was going to answer, but he did. "Luggage room at Spencer Street."

Wanda went ahead to after he'd got the box.

"Did you remove anything from the box before going to pass it on?"

"No."

Leo growled, believing it a lie, but Wanda knew she needed to ask exact questions.

"Was there an envelope with the box when you got it?"

"Yes."

"What was in it?"

"Paper," he said.

"Was that all?"

"All I saw."

"Where did you put the envelope?"

"In the post box."

Wanda tried another tack. "Where did you send it?"

"To the Post office."

"Who did you send it to?"

"Me."

"Poste Restante?"

"What?"

"For you to pick up there?"

"Yeah."

"Which post office did you send it to?"

"Kew."

"Did you use your own name?"

"Delaney, yeah."

Something prickled Wanda's mind, suggesting this was a lie, but she didn't say so aloud. She was watching Mickey's eyes, and they shifted ever so slightly towards where Leo was edging to the door. He was coming out of the trance, and she hadn't even given the command to do so. She was ready when he launched himself to the door and the promise of freedom.

Instead of taking the three strides towards the door, he fell heavily, tripped by Wanda's foot. Leo had only time to come to a fighting crouch. He straightened and said, "He's yours to play with. Enjoy yourself."

The door slammed shut as a raging Delaney leapt at it. He slammed the side of his fist against it in furious frustration. Then he remembered the woman.

"What did you do to me, bitch?"

"I finished the job the ruskies tried doing," Wanda said in the same flat tone she had been using all along. "They know where you sent the envelope."

Delaney shrugged. "Couldn't sell it anyway," he claimed. "Too hot. Just don't like foreigners thinking themselves my betters."

He strutted towards her. "But they gave you to me, and I intend to collect. Come here, bitch."

<u>Chapter 4</u>

Wanda didn't move as ordered. She turned, and eased into a fighting crouch, that caused Delaney to roar with laughter. He sprang at her, only to discover, she wasn't there, and felt a foot pushing him towards the floor. Things only got worse from there. Every attack he made was met by an unyielding defence, which repelled him back to the floor. The slip of a woman was like quicksilver, and he had already had a vicious pounding. Finally, he couldn't rise, or even react when Wanda rolled him onto his back, and stood over him. One foot resting on his genitals. Her quiet words went right into the primitive part of his mind, and if he had been a dog, he would have rolled over in submission.

"I know you were lying, you cockroach. That envelope, they won't find it at the Post Office, will they?"

"No."

"Where is it?"

"A mate has it."

"Try again. You wouldn't trust anyone with something worth so much."

"He doesn't know."

"Okay. What's his name?"

"Carson!"

He yelled that out, but Wanda sensed the lie. Still, she'd play along. His mind was picturing the actual place and she memorised the thought vision. "Carson who?"

"Jeremy Carson."

"Why him?"

"He has a safe."

"You trust him?"

"He don't dare sell it. I know too much about him."

"Well, now, Mickey – take your mind back to the very first

time you met him and tell me all about it."

This time, Mickey wasn't yelling, and the command on his mind was total. He told how they had met, how Carson, known then by another name, had tried to scam him. When challenged, Carson had offered a partnership, which had been lucrative indeed. Wanda suspected that Carson had earned a great deal more from it, but she didn't interrupt. The police had got interested after a few years, and that had ended.

"When did you meet again?" Wanda asked.

The man, now calling himself Carson, had offered him an unexpectedly satisfying task. A long term investment he had called it. Wanda was sickened, just listening to Mickey telling about it. Carson had only outlined the overall plan, and left the means to Mickey, but he must have known what Mickey was like.

Knowing some of the things Mickey had done, or she believed he had done, her questions were like arrows. Finally, she asked, "Why did you kill Ellie Hartley?"

This answer was unexpected. "They said the kid died. Carson didn't care. He reckoned he only needed one of the brats. So I took that one, and said I'd take care of the other. Got them to dress it in the outfit in the photo. Same ribbons and shoes and all. Thought it might be needed to convince the police stupid Maude was dangerous. Didn't need it though. The bitch was bonkers, going after any kid that wasn't attended."

"Why did you kill the little boy?"

"Stupid bitch thought it was a girl. That didn't fit the profile. Couldn't take it back."

Something akin to a dragon uncoiling writhed in Wanda's gut. A desire for the end of Delaney's life.

Wanda thought, "No! Not yet. There might be more to learn."

A sudden chill enveloped her, but it was directed at Delaney. "Make it soon!"

Wanda thought further. "Justice must be seen to be done. He might testify against Carson, to try to reduce his sentence.

I would let him." Then she envisioned the treatment prisoners got when it was known they had molested or killed children. Some of the intensity eased, but the sense that Mickey was a marked man strengthened. To that, Wanda simply thought, "Yes!"

That same something had the last word, as Wanda found her own voice speaking in a language she didn't understand. It felt old, but the meaning came to her. "You will never feel like a man again! You will tell the police everything they want to know – without trying to lie. If you are so proud of yourself you will boast of it."

Wanda added, "And you will never be able to look at me, or any woman, without recalling this total annihilation of your inner self." Accompanying those words, Wanda took a folded knife from her pocket and flicked out the blade, right in front of Delaney's face. "I like to make eunuchs of men like you."

She stepped over the quivering wreck, using the resting place of her foot as the first step. Her thought that her uncles had been watching was confirmed when the door was opened at her approach. She walked past them, blank faced, folding the knife and passing it to a startled Stephan. He hadn't realised she had taken it from him, and she didn't notice his sick expression. Without looking at anyone, she went to her room and made it to its tiny en-suite just in time, to throw up all the food she had recently eaten. Once she had calmed herself, she thought of the phone, and removed it from her pocket.

"Dav?"

"I'm here," he said quietly. "I couldn't hear all he said, but I got the bit about the envelope. I will tell Kelso to contact the post office. What was that about Carson?"

"Delaney was resisting me. I had him under, but he broke free. I am pretty certain that if he posted it, was lying about something. He said about Carson having it in his safe, but he was lying then too. I let it go, because the uncles will come back at me if they don't find what they want. If I mention Carson, they'll go question him. I think they will let me go with them. I want to get close to that scum."

"What else did Delaney say?"

"Later, Dav, Please?"

"Okay," David hesitated. "What do they plan to do with Delaney?"

"I don't know yet. I will try to suggest leaving him where the police can find him."

"Do you think you have worked off the second reaction?"

"Punishing Mickey was a good workout. The ape is solid. I feel okay at the moment. Oh, I should have mentioned, Maude helped Mickey collect that box from a locker at a big, busy train station and he posted the envelope from there."

"Do the uncles know that?"

"Delaney didn't actually say."

"Well done. Be careful!"

"I will. It's instinctive."

After rinsing her mouth, Wanda splashed water on her face, and checked how she looked in the mirror. Years of putting on a fake persona was the only asset that she had to hide her inner revulsion at what she had done. She wasn't sorry, though. Delaney was a parasite. Now though, she dare not betray weakness. Her uncles had been watching. They won't have heard all Delaney had said, but they would have seen him humiliated and at her mercy. She hoped they would respect her for the dangerous predator she had forced herself to be. Hearing a tapping on her door, she quickly combed her hair with a comb that had been in the en-suite, and took a deep breath. Her uncles would only see the posture of confidence, as they recalled what she had done.

"What is it?" she challenged as she went to open the door.

Leo stood there. "You finished with that offal?"

"For now," Wanda said casually. "Why? Have you thought of more questions?"

"No. Was he telling the truth?"

Wanda decided to be frank. "I believe he was telling the truth about posting it. But the details? I don't think he would even tell himself the truth. All I can say, I don't think he would have sent it to the house or got a PO Box. Filching the specs was likely a spur of the moment thing. The task force questioned his wife, who was staying at the house before his arrest. She didn't see the envelope there. I don't know if any of the others that helped him went back there or not. So if he posted it, he would have to do it to the Post Office to be held there for him."

"Well, Kew has a post office, and there is one in East Kew, and agencies in Belfield and across the river," Leo commented.

"Oh. I wasn't aware of all those places," Wanda admitted.

"No, I expect not," Leo sounded a little condescending. Wanda ignored it.

"So, what was that he was saying about someone with a safe?"

"It might be something," Wanda told him. "He could have posted it to the bloke and asked for it to be put in his safe. Do you know who this Carson is?"

"We'll find out," Leo said, sure of the fact. "Did you get what you wanted out of him?"

"More than I wanted to hear. He's scum. What are you going to do with him?"

"Keep him, for a bit longer, in case we don't find the envelope. What is the task force doing about it?"

Wanda shrugged. "They were hoping to find it at the house. They hadn't when I left. Seems that was a dud lead. As far as

I know, they'd only just found out the specs and stuff were missing."

"Will they keep looking?" Leo asked.

"Of course they will. Anyone could use those specs to build another prototype. That's what they don't want. They'd want to retrieve or destroy them."

"What are you planning to do now?"

Wanda decided Leo was a little uncertain about her. "Why? Want me to go?"

"What will the task force do if they know you are helping us?"

"Send me home. But you guys snatched me. They know I couldn't tell you much because I don't know much. If I escape by myself, they will want to know where I was being kept. Any suggestions?"

"I can arrange something. You might as well stay a bit longer. We might use you again."

"Kind of you. Must be because I have a knack with the newest of safes."

Leo growled, and looked about to explode again, but he composed himself. "That scum has made a mess in that room."

"Well don't expect me to clean up after him. Make him do it himself."

"Our women do as they are told."

"I'm not one of your women, and you had better remember you owe me again. I haven't forgotten how you punched me for no reason."

Leo took a step backward as Wanda went to brush past him. She resisted a grin at his reaction. Her act on Delaney had got to him too.

"Oh, and don't expect that scum to be docile. He'll take off as soon as you take your eyes off him. He'll want to get far, far away, now that I know his nasty little secrets. So if you don't want him here, like I said, dump him for the police to find. I want to see him locked up for the rest of his life. I hear that most people in prison, even the vilest of murderers, don't like blokes that muck with little kids, and when they hear how he killed a couple of little kids..."

Leo's growl, no longer aimed at her, was unfeigned.

"Exactly," Wanda announced. "He'll get his, no blame to you. By the way, did he have any ID on him?"

"Why?"

"Because unless you plan to break into those post offices, you will need ID to claim letters sent there for collection." Wanda made her tone deceptively meek.

"We'll fix something."

Wanda went out to the kitchen, and became the focus of three more pairs of eyes. In an instant she had summed up their body language. They were afraid of her. Good!

Gilroy stood and offered her a can of beer. She just shook her head and helped herself to a can of soft drink. She was going to be careful of anything they offered her. Somehow they had doped her before.

"How do we know you won't tell anyone about us?"

"I don't have to. They already know. What the local police don't know is my unfortunate heritage, which I decided was severed once I heard your sire was dead."

"You helped us. They won't like that."

"Don't assume you are that far ahead of them," Wanda said what she would have considered obvious. "Look, they think I was your prisoner. They don't know me that well. If they see Mickey like I left him, who would think I could do that? If I happen to leak some of the stuff I learnt, well, I just happened to overhear it. If some of that helps them with their other Mickey related investigations, well, I'll be the saviour in disguise."

She glanced at Eduardo and Stephan, before returning her attention to Gilroy. "Okay, you can be assured that I will not be telling anyone about what I did today. If they find out, I will be painted with the same brush as the rest of The Family, and I have been managing quite well without you, thank you very much."

She put the unopened can down on the table and walked outside.

Leaving the uncles was a deliberate ploy to make them believe she was not interested in what they did next. And in fact, she didn't want to know what they planned. She had already given David the important info, about the specs. He and Kelso would be all over that. If Gilroy wanted the post offices checked, he couldn't do anything right away. If he was smart, and he was supposedly the new brains of that branch of the family, they would drop the whole thing. Their buyers had fled, and may not even be interested in just the plans, unless they had someone who could craft a new prototype. However, they may even know someone who could. The Family had a very great reach.

The problem was, now, that their credibility had taken a severe blow. They needed a show of competence to erase that. She had no intention of being a part of that. She would just keep using them to find out things she wanted to know. Fair exchange... and she just hoped she could hold out against the ominous shaky feeling that was returning.

An angry Leo stamped into the kitchen. Martin's cousins took one look at him and decided they were no longer hungry, and went directly to one of their rooms.

"The bastard got away," Leo announced. "Nik is fuming."

"I told you he'd take off," Wanda said calmly. "Did you find what you wanted?"

"No. Nik looked in the post office data base and found no likely mention of it. If he sent it right after he stole the unit, it should have been there. Even if he sent it to his mate, and the mate sent it on, it should have been. We took the bastard to the station – it's called Southern Cross Station now, and looked in the locker he had a key for. It was full of clothes. While we were looking he took off."

Clever, Wanda had to admit to herself. She tried to think what Delaney would do now. Consider the specs a lost cause and hot foot it out of the area? She felt in her pocket and fast dialled David. Her phone volume was right down, so if he answered, no one would hear and he would soon realise he needed to listen.

"I want that bastard," Leo stated. "Any idea where he might go?"

"Did he get paid for the heist?" Wanda asked.

"A retainer, the rest was due on delivery, but he let himself be caught."

"Well, he hasn't been out of jail long. Probably hasn't that much money available. He'll be wanting some."

"We'll check out his mate Carson. I'll suggest that to Nik. You! Do you have what you need to open stuff?" Wanda bristled at his tone. "All but the couple of tools that dropped from my pocket when you humped me away from the house like I was a sack of potatoes."

"Good enough. You'll make do if you are as good as you reckon you are."

Wanda kept her annoyance in check. Her strength was to seem to be in control all the time, and she reminded herself she did want to get into Carson's place. She only half listened to Leo talking to his brother. Her main attention was planning what she wanted to do once she was at Carson's place. Once they were finished there, she was parting company with her unwanted relatives.

Leo had started pacing once he finished his call, and jumped when Gilroy arrived unannounced.

"Calm down Leo," he said immediately. "I have a lead on the location of Kemple. I sent Jos off to get him. He might know what his mate did with the envelope. Eduardo, if he finds him, I want you to be there when Jos questions him. However, I think checking on this Carson is still worthwhile. We can make sure he knows not to help Delaney in any way."

Eduardo looked relieved. Gilroy looked at Leo. "You can drive us. Keep an eye out for trouble."

That seemed agreeable to Leo.

"Stephan, I want you and our niece to come with me. I want to keep this on a nice friendly basis. Carson might have nothing to do with this business, and we don't want him involving the police."

Wanda just nodded, thinking Carson wouldn't dare do that. However, a vengeful Delaney, if he recalled what he said, might send the police there, to get back at his tormentors.

Gilroy went on. "Do you two think you can get in and scout his house without him seeing you?"

Stephan nodded, Wanda copied him. "Good. I want you to go in. I will wait twenty minutes and arrive at the front door. You two can join me once I am inside. I will want his safe opened, either by his invitation, or by my insistence."

"Are you expecting us to find anything in particular?"

"Other safes, potential hiding places. If we don't finish tonight, one of you can go back again later. However, before we go, do you have a way to make that outfit look less like you just got it at an op-shop?"

"Well, sorry. Next time you abduct me I'll make sure I have a case of clothes."

"There's an iron in the laundry. Appearances are important."

Wanda had a vivid flashback from when she was seventeen, and it reminded her of the stakes now. What she was agreeing to, without coercion, was illegal. That she was sending a warning of her intent to David and a former policeman meant she couldn't claim to have been made to do it, and wasn't currently drug addled.

When his phone rang, David listened before speaking, and heard Leo Tatarovich ranting. He listened carefully and passed on what he heard. Kelso acted on the information by passing it to Kingly. The conversation made sense, since David had made notes of what he had heard earlier.

The result was, that a perimeter was being set up around Carson's house, waiting for Delaney, or the Family members to approach. Kelso told David to come with him to be nearer the action. He had arranged with one of Carson's neighbours, for the use of a room in the front. The neighbour, a sensible woman in her sixties, accepted his story of watching for someone who was threatening Carson. She professed no particular like or dislike of him, and saw them settled, then kept out of the way.

To help the time pass, Kelso asked, "What else did Wanda get from Delaney?"

"She said she'd tell me later. I think it was pretty nasty. She finished with him and had just thrown up."

David kept the rest of his belief to himself. She had probably done to him, something like she had done to her unlamented grandfather. Something she had only admitted to him, and her cousin was the only witness.

Kelso spoke again a little while later. "What's making you edgy?"

"Wanda told me her uncles had doped her. She reacts oddly to a lot of drugs. At first is seems only that they wear of faster than expected, but later, some make her hyper, and possibly to hallucinate and there are some particularly frightening things she could remember and react against. The second reaction hasn't hit her yet, but I am not ready to say it won't this time."

"How long do you think she plans to stay with her relatives?" Kelso asked then.

"She wanted a go at Delaney," David admitted, but Kelso had known that. "She also wants to get close to Carson and try to read him. I think, she is going along with the relatives, as they will allow her to do that."

"Do you think he has the envelope?"

"I don't know."

"What about Delaney, do you think he will come here?"

"No. He threw Carson's name at them, I think as a ruse to get them off his case. He's being looked for by the police. He must know that. He's had a going over by The Family, and has to know they will still be after him for that damned envelope. If that was a ruse, to try to get out of remand, and he can't produce it, he will want to get away as soon as he can. He might try to twist Carson for money. But I don't think he will come in person."

"I think it's a long shot," Kelso finally admitted. "But it's all we have right now."

"I wish we could bug Carson's phone," David muttered.

"Well, we can't. Do you want me to get all units to look out for Wanda? In case she does intend to head back tonight?"

After a moment of thought, David nodded.

Episode 14

Carson Under Pressure

Chapter 1

"Does Wanda have a plan?" Kelso asked. He was taking the first watch of the street.

"Apart from getting close to Carson? I don't think she plans too exactly. She works with what she gets. Her instincts are very good."

"What about when she is affected by drugs?" Kelso prodded.

"Every other time, like when we were testing the effects, she did maintain a thread of control."

"Let's hope that holds true," Kelso said quietly. "And let's hope Delaney is desperate enough to come here and try to see Carson. It will give us a reason to go in there."

They fell silent. David thinking, while Kelso watched. After a while, David said, "You know, there is one aspect of the post idea we didn't consider. I know Wanda said a PO Box was unlikely, but didn't I tell you that Kemple senior had one?"

"Already checked. I had records give me a list of Delaney's known associates, and I had them run through the post office records. Kemple did have one, still does for a while longer, but is empty. But that's not to say he didn't collect something recently. Like after he got out on Tuesday. We've got him on a list of people of interest, but he must be lying low."

Kelso suddenly put a hand to his ear. "Roberts has just reported all lights have gone out at the back of Carson's place." Moments later, the same happened at the front, and Kelso reported it via a collar mike.

He added after a moment, "Someone has just come out and got into a brown car." Through the collar mike he requested police to follow and apprehend the driver.

"I wonder if he is expecting trouble and sending his housekeeper out of the way," David aired his thought.

"Let's wait and see," Kelso suggested. "Have you got your phone out?"

"Yes." He was expecting Wanda to have it streaming sound to him, as she had before.

Ten minutes later, a short burst of static had them both listening tensely.

"Give us ten minutes," an accented voice said.

A softer, woman's voice countered that. "No, allow the full twenty. Carson is ultra-security conscious."

"How do you know him?"

"I got that out of his daughter."

Kelso spoke quietly. "All units, move in to perimeter one."

Then, although they listened hard, neither Kelso nor David heard anything from the phone, until a loud phone ringing tone emanated from it. They both jumped, but then they heard Carson's voice, almost like he was right beside them. He answered the phone only with his surname, and was then quiet for several minutes. Then he exploded. Thinking he was alone in the house, he didn't moderate his voice.

"No! You listen to me. I don't want to be involved in problems you made for yourself. What do you expect me to do with your foreign gangsters? You haven't given me a thing and I will tell them as much. As for me giving you money, unless you come here and tell them what they want, you can forget it. Besides, I don't have 50 thou here...No, I haven't forgotten, but the investment hasn't matured yet, and you are putting all that in jeopardy. I have to keep my image clean."

Whatever the caller was saying, it echoed from Carson's phone as an indistinct murmur.

"Is that damn thing worth it? Can you sell it? Tell me where you sent it and I will tell them. That had better be the truth, Mickey, or you can say goodbye to your money. Okay, I am trusting you and I'll organise your money, but that will make us even. Don't try for more, ever!"

A pause with more unclear words.

"That will take even longer. I can get 10 thou, and send the rest to a bank account. Do you have one? I told you, I don't keep that much here. I'll have to go to the bank, tomorrow, when it opens."

A pause.

"No don't come here. Look, go to Long Lonny's. Tell him I sent you. I will call you there."

The sound of Carson slamming down the phone came clearly. Five minutes later, the door chime echoed through the house. A full minute passed before they heard Carson's echoing footsteps moving away. David wished the phone could follow Carson, but that would mean Wanda moving away from whatever vantage point she had found.

"Yes, he said you would be coming," Carson said calmly, his voice getting louder. "And I resent him making me the fall guy in this. Come through to my office. Delaney called me just as I was about to go up to bed."

A pause, then the voice was softer. "Sit down if you wish. Do you want something to drink?"

Only because the house was so quiet, did the low voices carry to the phone.

"Did Delaney tell you what we wanted?" That voice carried a faint accent.

"In detail, no. I didn't want anything to do with his schemes. He just said you were after an envelope that he considered worth 50 thousand dollars. He told me to tell you I had posted it on, after he had it sent here."

"And to where did you send it," the accented voice asked, still pleasant and polite.

"I didn't, Carson said bluntly. "Nor do I have it, or seen it. Now, before you take affront, you would do well to believe me when I say that you can't believe anything Delaney says. As I mentioned, he rang me not long before you got here. He may have tried earlier, but I was out."

"So where did he tell you to say he had posted it to?" Gilroy's voice had a slightly bantering tone.

"To the Post Office Agency in East Kew. But he said he used his wife's name, not his own. It might be under her maiden name, Hartley, first name Maude."

"And you don't believe that is the truth?" Gilroy asked.

"I'd be very surprised if it was."

There was silence for a while, and outside in the car, David murmured, "Carson's a cool one, but he doesn't know who he is talking to."

It seemed that he was about to find out.

"I believe that Delaney is trying to twist both of us," Gilroy remarked. "The envelope contains information worth half a million dollars, but only in a very restricted market. I am surprised that he did not tell you to demand money for the information."

Carson continued his blunt answers. "He did, but my business makes me a decent living, and I don't want to be an accessory to his crimes."

"I understand," Gilroy said suavely. "However, you might understand why I must insist on searching here to be sure you are telling the truth."

"What? I have no reason to lie to you and you have no right to insist on a search." Carson's voice had risen a little in pitch.

"We are both business men, Mr Carson. We each have our own secrets and I am not interested in yours. A quick check, and if we don't find it, we go." Gilroy snapped his fingers, and a baritone voice spoke.

"The rest of the house is clear," Stephan Tatarovich reported, startling Carson into standing up.

"You searched my house!" Carson exclaimed.

"Naturally," Gilroy replied. "Now will you open my safe, or will I have Stephan do it?"

"No, I won't."

Stephan knew what was expected on him, and moved further into the room. Carson moved to one side, as if protecting his safe.

"Sit down, Mr Carson. Neither of us want the police coming here as the result of a gunshot. Where is your safe?"

Carson moved aside and Stephan walked to look behind a painting.

"Predictable," he murmured. "One of the newest models. I will need to blow it."

"No!" Carson objected, forgetting that the noise would draw the unwanted attention, his visitor had mentioned.

"Then open it?" Gilroy suggested.

Carson went and sat silently. Gilroy snapped his fingers again. "Well, if you must be stubborn."

Wanda entered without fanfare and went directly to the safe, keeping her face away from Carson as much as she could. After five minutes, with only vague sounds, Wanda announced, "It's open, you can look for what you want. I'm going to check these panels. I think they hide cupboards."

"How did you do that?" Carson exclaimed, disbelieving his eyes. Wanda didn't answer, just re-hid two tools.

Stephan took the small gun Gilroy had produced, and kept watching Carson as Wanda found and quickly flicked through the contents behind the panels. Gilroy searched the safe, taking everything out, including a large sum of money, then carefully replaced everything, then closed and locked the safe.

"Thank you, Mr Carson," Gilroy said. "I don't think we will need to meet again. Perhaps you will call me if our mutual problem contacts you. We will be happy to deal with him."

"I'll do that," Carson promised. "I would be happy to be rid of him. I will see you all out. Where did that woman go?"

"She wasn't too happy to come with us. I believe she is making her point and is gone already."

Wanda hadn't gone far. She intended to retrieve her phone and had slipped out, into a nook she had noticed when scouting the downstairs areas. She didn't know how Gilroy would react to her vanishing, but she had done what they wanted. In any case, she had her own agenda and that was to wait and listen to Carson's private reaction to his visitors.

She wasn't surprised when he went and checked every window and door on the ground floor, and set the night alarm on them. He disappeared upstairs and Wanda followed part way up the stairs, saw reflected lights going on and off as door were opened and closed. Then she heard water running and ghosted back down stairs to Carson's office. She reached in to where she had placed her phone. It wasn't there.

She risked using her tiny torch, to check behind the low bookcase in case it had fallen down there. Then she crouched down to feel the floor under it.

The hand that grabbed her was rough and brutal.

"So, you went off before the others, did you?" Carson snarled. "You are going to wish you had. How did you know the combination of my safe? Did those young bastards that are harassing me, tell you?"

Wanda decided to say nothing. He dragged her to the chair where Gilroy had sat and shoved her into it. She was prepared to spring up and run when he pulled a gun on her.

"I'm going to call the police, and tell them I caught an intruder.

What do you say to that?"

"Go ahead," Wanda invited, smirking. "Will you be mentioning your earlier visitors, or are you scared of them?"

"Are you?"

"No. I did what they wanted of me, and decided it was time to part company."

"Why were you recording the discussion?" He held up her now closed phone.

"To have something on those bastards. They grabbed me when I was working for the Atlas Task Force. They are the ones I don't want to think I deliberately ducked out on."

"Are you a policeman?"

Wanda laughed. "Hell no, I'm their 'security expert'. I used to crack safes for a living."

"I find that hard to believe," Carson sneered.

"So did all the cops in New York," Wanda smirked. "But I didn't give them a demonstration. Anyway, that recording won't implicate you. You were telling the truth about that Neanderthal, Delaney, weren't you?"

Carson's face relaxed as he thought back over the conversation. However, Wanda was far from relaxed. Her whole body was beginning to twitch.

"I think you should let me leave," Wanda told him as calmly as she could. "Or you might discover how I put the fear of hell into Mickey Delaney. Surely you have guessed he wants to leave town."

"No. You stay right there," Carson kept the gun aimed her way, but his free hand was moving towards the phone on his desk. He glanced down for an instant.

Carson felt the air leave his lungs after a foot rammed him in the chest. He could not help himself as the woman shoved him so he fell over his desk. As soon as he could, he straightened and stumbled out to see where the woman had gone.

The dark figure was headed for the back door. He almost yelled as the figure headed straight for the low built up ledge around the Jacuzzi. But at the last minute the figure jumped onto the ledge and began to trot along it. He began to raise the gun just as the front door chimes echoed through the huge hall way again.

Carson glanced at the front door, for just a moment. He looked back just as the dark figure fell sideways. He heard the thud and ran to look. The woman wasn't moving. He stared for a long moment to be sure, and then went to answer the door. He felt in his pocket for the phone, having thought of a way to use the recording, but it wasn't there.

"Hello, Sir. Sorry to bother you at this late hour, but we have had a report of an escaped criminal in this area, and we are checking all the houses. Are you here alone?"

Kelso had the speech down pat, so David merely stood quietly, seeing what he could behind Carson."

"Yes, I am alone. My wife and daughter are visiting relatives and it is my housekeeper's night off. Surely you don't think this person came in here? I haven't been home long, but I have had the alarm system on."

"That wouldn't stop Mickey Delaney," David stated bluntly. "This is a big house. He could easily get in and hide."

"I assure you, if any of the sensors were tripped, I would have received a text message."

"Delaney is a dangerous individual," Kelso stressed. "We don't wish him to remain free. We have no desire to place any individual in this neighbourhood at risk, either. The Dog squad are on their way here to check the yards and gardens. We could accompany you on a tour of the house, to be sure, and then we will have to move on."

A helicopter was circling the area, and had a spotlight focussed on the area of Riverpark. That seemed to convince Carson that the visit wasn't a ruse. He had tensed, but then relaxed and nodded abruptly.

"Yes, good of you. Come in."

David, adept at reading body reactions, observed and catalogued Carson's reactions to consider later. The man had been lying, he and Kelso knew he'd had guests, and been home all evening. That Wanda had been in the house, they knew, and she might still be. The light cordon of watchers around the house had not seen her leave. His reading of Carson suggested he knew she was still in the house and was afraid she would be found. His relaxing, could have been because he had thought of a way to use the fact if she was found.

"I didn't notice anything amiss when I came in," Carson lied smoothly. "This is the main bedroom," he said as he moved them to his right. I do keep some fairly valuable items, my spare watch and my wife's lesser jewellery in a locked drawer in here."

Doors came off the grandiose entrance hall, David guessed the office was to the left.

Carson stood back and let the two men, he assumed to be policemen, look for themselves. He gave the virtual tour of his house by mentioning what each room was. All the time, he positioned himself between them and the Jacuzzi. He let his unwelcome guests check in wardrobes and under beds. When they were exploring the laundry, downstairs bathroom and the kitchen, he risked a look at where the woman had fallen. His gut knotted – she wasn't there. While he thought he saw a trace of red, some water had collected in the bottom that hadn't been there before. While it was a relief in one way that the woman wasn't there, the fact alarmed him. His guests returned.

David remarked. "Your back door was unlocked. Did you do that when you came home?"

Carson didn't hide his surprise. He had set the perimeter alarms, he should have heard an alarm if the woman had gone. He said as much to his visitors.

"We closed it and locked it," David said. "I advise you to have the system checked first thing tomorrow. I think perhaps Delaney might have been here, hiding, but left when he heard we were to search."

"We should continue. Just to be sure," Kelso directed.

Carson took them to each door in sequence, arriving outside his office last. "My office is through that door. I have a safe there and sometimes keep cash there. Then we have four bedrooms and a bathroom upstairs."

He hadn't had time to straighten his desk, and so feigned surprise at the subtle mess.

"It seems that your concerns were correct, Sir," he admitted to Kelso. "I'm in your debt. I was thinking of working more tonight. I might have been attacked, or forced to open my safe."

Kelso studied the room, knowing David was as well. "Does anything look to be missing?"

David abruptly began coughing, needing Kelso to delay a bit longer.

"David? Are you alright?" Kelso, not expecting this was alarmed.

He held up a hand, and managed to say, "You are not a smoker, are you, Sir?"

Carson shook his head, as David's coughing spasm erupted again.

"Sorry," David managed. "I just need some water."

"I'll get some," Carson offered.

"No, No. You finish checking so that we can go. I know the way, if you don't mind."

Carson waved him out, his gaze lingering until David was out of sight. "That sounded bad."

"Yes," Kelso agreed, thoughtfully. "I will give you my card, in case you discover something missing. Now, I think we should still check upstairs."

The coughing, still audible upstairs, slowly eased off. When Kelso came down, he found David leaning over the sink, breathing deeply, in and out.

"You've been doing too much," Kelso admonished. "I don't think you have recovered as much as you think."

"Maybe you are right," David seemed reluctant to admit.

"I will call for a relief team to replace us and I will see you go home," Kelso directed, before apologising again for disturbing Carson. "Are you comfortable staying here tonight? Or would you like a police watch in case Delaney returns?"

"Surely he won't. He'll be running from all the activity."

"Well, I can't say one way or the other. However, the police interest will still be in the area. However, if you do have any concerns, you can call the number on the card I gave you. I am no longer a policeman, but I do liaise closely with them. Thank you. We will see ourselves out."

The first thing Kelso did when they were back at the car was to call Des Kingley and report.

"No, he was alone in the house. We didn't challenge him, but he lied about being in the house most of the day, and he didn't mention his visitors. Our agent was not still in there. Any word from the cordon?"

Kelso frowned as Kingley reported no sign of Wanda. "Yes, I will be back at my place in fifteen minutes. I will see you there."

Kelso started the car, and moved out onto the main part of the road. "So, what can you add?"

"Let me think this out."

"Do you think we should have followed those Russians?"

"No. We know where they all are staying," David said absently. "Besides, we know Delaney called to warn Carson of them. There wasn't time for him to hide anything after the call. They didn't find what they wanted or Wanda would have given us a code phrase. Gilroy's comment suggested she ducked out before them, we assumed she had her phone and turned it off. What if she had it placed in the office and had to duck back and get it? That is she didn't want Carson to know she was streaming the call, so had to get it after he went out too."

"I can't see how you came to that idea, but go on with your supposition."

Chapter 4

David considered all he had observed.

"I don't know what then, but Carson was uptight when we arrived at his door. I don't think it was because we claimed Delaney was in the area, but it might have been, even though we heard through Wanda's phone that he told him to stay away. He may have been thinking Delaney had called from close by, then decided with the obvious police presence, and the helicopter, he wouldn't stay around."

"I agree, Carson had something on his mind, other than his unwelcome visitors. Ideas? Do you think he knew Wanda was still there?"

"I hate to say it, but yes. Did you notice how he always kept between us, and the Jacuzzi?"

"I did, but only until we came out from the kitchen. Is that why you had your convenient coughing fit?"

David chuckled. "That and to place a listening device. Put the radio onto FM channel 2. I programmed it into the radio."

"That's not legal," Kelso reproved.

"Who's to know? We won't be using it to get evidence on him. I know that won't be allowed. We might, however, get more of a hint of something we can check from another direction."

Kelso said no more on the subject. "Find anything?"

"Wanda's phone was in the Jacuzzi, and there was a trace of reddish water in the bottom of it."

"Do you think he did something to her?" Kelso almost braked sharply.

"If he did, it wasn't incapacitating," David allowed. "Someone did go out the back way, bypassing the security. What I think might have happened is that she might have fallen, or apparently fallen, and Carson saw it and expected her to still be in there."

"So, she used us as cover to sneak out. Then why didn't she

go to the first police unit she saw?"

David was silent.

"David?"

"I hadn't thought of that. I was thinking that as she didn't have her phone we'd have to wait to hear from her. Damn! Do you recall that reaction I mentioned, she was managing to control it, but — if she was a bit hurt from say a fall, it might have triggered."

"Everyone was asked to look out for her," Kelso reminded him. "Should I warn them about a bad reaction to an illegally administered substance?"

Reluctantly, David nodded. To cover his worry, he leant forward to turn the radio volume to full.

"What's the range of that thing?" Kelso asked. "Could we hear it from my place?"

They both heard some static.

"Closer is better," David said. "Pull in!"

The radio came to life. Carson's voice came clearly.

"Victoria, it's me, Jeremy. Yes, yes, I am too dear...Victoria! Shut up and listen. I want you and the girl to head back to Melbourne on the bus tomorrow. Yes, tomorrow! I have booked two tickets on the bus. You can pick them up at the depot. When you get into Melbourne, take a taxi to the hotel on Collins Street. I have also booked a room there, in your name. Stay there, and keep the girl there until I come and get you. Understand?"

There was a pregnant silence.

"Victoria, just do as I say. I have everything under control. Yes, yes, do that. I am sure Abbie won't refuse to get herself pampered."

"Well, well, contrary to what he just said, I think Carson is off balance," Kelso remarked. "Thanks to Delaney setting those

Russians on him out of the blue, and then our little visit to him.”

“I’d like to know what he’s up to,” David muttered.

Carson finished his call to his wife, then began another. “Lonny? Is Mickey there? Put him on.”

“Mickey, you owe me some favours if you want that 50K. No, you listen. You set those foreigners on me and I have had the police checking house to house for you…I know that! I’m sure that was only an excuse. But doing that has put the whole scheme in jeopardy. So just lie low…I’ll get your money, but I have to be extra careful, and I may have to delay if I am being watched.”

The radio went silent, but Kelso wasn’t ready to rush off. Fifteen minutes passed in silence.

“Des will be waiting for us. We will be told if Carson goes out again tonight,” Kelso suggested. Why don’t you call Fred and have him activate my other watchers, and tell Des we are on the way.”

David complied, and Kelso began heading back home.

“I wonder why Carson wants them back tomorrow.”

“Maybe they are all going to relocate?” Kelso proposed as a way to get ideas flowing.

“No, he would just have to go join them and leave from there.”

“What about all the stuff in his house?” Kelso countered.

“True, he’d not want to leave anything that might incriminate him. I think he no longer trusts having his wife and daughter out of his sight.”

“Or he wants them within reach,” Kelso twisted the idea.

“Well, we know he has something going on with Mickey Delaney, or did have,” David changed tacks. “Now, Mickey was married to Maude Hartley, and we have a supposition that Carson is after the Hartley fortune. He has the birth certificate of one of the girls, which is suggestive. He tells his wife Abbie is his daughter by some dead ex-girlfriend. If it was Maude, and he considered her being committed as being out of the way for good, why didn't he approach the Hartley lawyers?"

"Deniability," Kelso said flatly. "He can pretend he didn't know Maude was a Hartley, or that he assumed they wouldn't care for a bastard to the name, or a dozen other reasons."

"And let time cloud what really happened," David added. "I know you told me that no one expected Maude to be released. Maybe Carson has only just found out that she was."

"I don't think that's it," Kelso interrupted. "I think he waited this long for a reason."

"Well, it couldn't have been from the find at the scout house. That wasn't planned by him, or Delaney." David yawned. "Let's allow the ideas to simmer."

David's head was aching by the time he reached Kelso's house. Inside, Kingley was seated in a lounge chair, waiting for them. The chief superintendent rose, concerned by the pallour of the face of the young American.

"I have all cars looking out for your wife. Can you tell me more about how she might be acting?"

"I'll do my best," David agreed, and Kelso nodded.

"Then sit down, before you fall down," Kingley directed.

Once he had, David explained what he knew from previous instances and summing up with, "I tend to think she keeps acting on the last coherent thought she has before the reaction takes over. I am sure she was in Carson's house, and used our arrival to leave. If she was only thinking of getting away, she is likely to get out and keep going, in whatever direction she was headed. And if she didn't want to be seen, she won't be."

"What if she is approached?" Kingley asked.

"Depends if the person who does is friendly or not. I am hoping she will wear herself out and zonk."

Kingley filed that for future reference, and moved on to more official business.

"Tell me about your visit to Carson's place."

Kelso gave the basics of their visit, and then David added his observations. Information was exchanged, some of it highly confidential, and only shared because of Kelso's former police rank, and that David was part of the Task Force.

"So, do you think Carson knows anything about the data on that prototype?" Kingley asked bluntly.

"No," David was equally blunt. "I think Mickey was trying to mislead the group who visited Carson."

"I don't want Mickey getting away," Kingley growled. "I will have the name Long Lonny run through records, but it may not give us anything. Bad enough that Delaney was spotted at Southern Cross station but was gone before we could get anyone there. The CCTV footage showed him with a couple of hefty types, looking in one of the lockers. It wasn't the one where we found the envelope though."

"Ah," David exclaimed, looking up. "Then you found them?"

"Indeed. Kemple was followed to a café, yesterday afternoon." David nodded, he knew that much. Kingley went on, "I had a plainclothes man take over from Fred. He went in, checked Kemple was still there and came out to watch. Apparently though, Kemple slipped out the back way. We had a bit of luck, because Kemple used a taxi to go from there to the local post office. He had a box there. He was just in time to be able to pick the envelope up inside. It had been too big to fit in his box. The CCTV in there showed him with it. He took another taxi to Southern Cross Station and arranged a new locker to put it in. We organised a search warrant, and extracted it. Commander Britten is in the process of having the contents modified so there are deliberate errors. He'll have the envelope returned to the locker, which is currently being watched, as we expect Delaney to come for it when he is about to take off."

Then Kelso delicately mentioned the listening device David had placed in Carson's house. Kingley gave his former superior a glare. "Is this standard practice for the Task Force?"

David answered, "It won't come back at you as nothing was recorded, just listened to. It gives us information to work on."

"So what did it tell you?" Kingley asked, his voice perfectly neutral.

"That I don't think Mickey will leave before Carson comes up with the 50K he was promised for whatever he did," David opined.

"Carson's worth a lot more than that," Kingley admitted.

"And if those two who claim he is their father can be believed, all of it was from one scam or another," David said. "We need to talk to them. If they are legit in their claim, they may be the link we are looking for with the Hartley business."

"I still don't see Carson the way you do, David, but I will play along. However, my main concern is recapturing Delaney and finding out how those people you call The Family forged the papers to get him released."

"Catching Delaney is one of our main concerns too," Kelso assured his friend. "And another is to find out why a stalwart member of the public with an impeccable public image, has anything to do with a vicious, ruthless type like him."

"You would need to prove the connection," Kingley warned, mildly.

"Has there been any response to the newspaper articles?" Kelso asked.

Kingley grunted. "Some. The usual money grubbers and cranks. The more likely ones are being looked into. If Carson read it, he should have reacted. After all, it is your contention that Jeremy Carson believes he has one of the lost Hartley heirs."

"He's had a lot of other things on his mind," David said maliciously. "But maybe that is why he wants his daughter back in Melbourne." He grimaced as his head began to pound with the returning headache. "That reminds me. I spoke to a nurse while I was still incarcerated this morning. She said something about adoptions, 12 years ago being sealed so neither birth parent not adoptive parents knew who the other was. I do wonder whether people who adopted back then and are still in the area, will come forward. It might be they haven't told their child they were adopted."

"There is only one, we want to react," Kelso reminded him.

"I have had police aides checking on adoptions from back then, nothing stands out. We have the family names of adoptive parents, but that doesn't help much. However, back then there were a couple of shady adoption agencies, and their records can't be trusted at all," Kingley informed them.

David recalled, "Carson said he didn't have to adopt his daughter, she was his, the mother had said before she died."

"And the Department has no record of any such child," Kingley confirmed. He stood up, preparing to leave, "Keep up the good work. David, we will call if we have any word of your wife."

David didn't sleep well. His headache was defying the tablets he had been given, and he was more worried about Wanda than he was letting on. He had come to the conclusion that the headache was linked to her. If he hadn't been feeling so bad, he would have been out, driving around, looking for her.

In the morning it had eased, but if Wanda was better, why hadn't she got in touch? She knew his number, and Kelso's home and mobile, she carried change for a pay phone, although he hadn't noticed many of them around. Sure, he had Wanda's phone, and he was glad Kingley hadn't realised it had been recording earlier.

He wanted to get out, looking for his wife, afraid of the state she was in, but as soon as he suggested it, Kelso vetoed it.

"You need to take time out to rest, or you will be fit for nothing. Kingley has the police watching out for her, and they can be in more places than you, and know their areas better."

"I need to do something," David insisted.

"I will see if we can have access to some old case files. I recall something about illegal adoption services now that Des mentioned them. Maybe if you go through the statements and transcripts, you will find a useful lead to follow."

"How long will that take?" David asked.

"I'll get onto Des. You might also go over the transcripts of the calls that came in about the newspaper articles. You and your wife have an uncanny instinct for finding clues."

"I'll start with them. Do they have the calls recorded too?"

"Yes, and you might be able to get access online."

Chapter 6

After two groups of unwelcome visitors, sleep was far from Carson's mind. Mickey Delaney had too much nerve – putting him in the firing line of those foreigners. He had always known Mickey was dangerous, but so far, if paid well enough, he'd come through. He had no scruples. This time though, he'd got mixed up in something well out of his league. The foreigners had really put the wind up him. If they fouled up his long planned coup, Mickey wouldn't live to regret it.

However, if he had read those strangers right, he had convinced them that he knew nothing. Thank the heavens that he had removed all his important records already. And it was unbelievable how that woman had opened his safe. Too bad he didn't dare mention her.

He wasn't completely sure whether the foreigners owned her or not. Best say nothing. Those foreigners didn't need official interest in their business any more than he did. The woman probably wouldn't be a problem. She'd been off her head, stoned. She'd looked pretty bad when she'd fallen. He had thought she was dead – but she couldn't have been in a good state. If she was ducking out on the foreigners, they'd be after her. She can't have wanted anyone else to see her if she had crawled away when the doorbell went.

The visitors, he hadn't let on that he'd recognised the old policeman, what had been their game? Had he been singled out? He would send Mrs Butterworth out to see if anyone else mentioned having their place looked through. Maybe it wasn't just him.

Just more to be annoyed about, thanks to Mickey Delaney. Still, they would have noticed nothing suspicious.

Carson considered reneging on his promise to Delaney, but if he did he'd never get any peace. But 50 grand now, was cheap

187

compared to what he expected to get when Abbie was confirmed as the Hartley heir. Trouble was, Delaney wanted cash, not a bank transfer. That would be a problem. He only kept 10 grand in his safe – for emergencies.

Anyone investigating him, like the Trustees, would find him withdrawing forty grand in cash unusual, if not downright suspicious. Unless he had a logical reason to arrange it.

He'd sleep on it. He had a busy day tomorrow.

Long used to reading people's body language, Carson had a knack for homing in on their doubts and providing the needed reassurance. The couple from the Department of Human Services had gone away completely satisfied by his trustworthiness. They believed he had not known who Maude was, all those years ago. He had also subtly implied that if he had been criminally minded, he would have contacted the family's trustees back when he had picked up the girl. They had not found records of the event, but what could he say? He claimed that was what he had been told they were. And since then, he had looked after the girl like she was his own kid. Well, she was his, and he had given her the best he could provide. He had been doing well enough. Now he just had to coach Victoria on her part – what to say and what not to say.

He'd wait for evening, after Victoria and the girl had settled into the hotel, and then go to see them. He wasn't sure how Abbie would react. She had been behaving like an ungrateful bitch recently. Hopefully, the other week would have shocked some sense into her, and she would do as she was told now.

The Hartley Trustees would get in touch next, he guessed. The advantage of waiting this long was that all the old retainers had retired or moved on. Those there now, would all have been hired in recent years.

If they called before Friday, he would just say his wife and daughter were on the way back from a family visit up north.

Satisfied that matter was under control, Carson turned his mind to other aspects of his businesses. He still felt a shiver of unease about the previous night. He did not need any nosy body looking at his business. He decided then and there to take the advice of the old cop's offsider, and got the security company out to check the system.

He got through to one of the consultants, and was gratified by their alarm at what he told them. They should be.

He was mollified when they sent a technician out right away. This time, he knew everything would be set up properly.

The technician from the safe company, came out with satisfying promptness to change the lock for him. They had assured him that the woman must have had the original combination. Possibly the rental agency looking after the house had known it and told someone.

The anticipation of the lucrative return of his decade long investment brought a faint smile to Carson's face. The real humour was that this was as close to legitimate as any of his businesses had got. He wouldn't need to duck out and start again elsewhere. Over twenty five years of successfully running investment swindles of various kinds, had allowed him to build a substantial nest egg. After this last one, he could retire to the Caribbean, or some other haunt of the rich and famous.

Abbie was the sole remaining Hartley. That dumpy simpleton, Maude, would be no problem. After all this time, she'd not remember him or the name he'd used. She'd not really recalled him at the time. All she had wanted was to be laid and have a kid. In any case, it would be easy to make an accident happen to her, once Abbie was confirmed as her daughter, and her trust transferred.

A simple DNA test would do it. Just as it had proved that

Abbie's one time twin was dead. And that had been an unexpected bonus to have been discovered just now.

At least Mickey had no qualms about that. Personally, he hadn't wanted two kids to deal with. Kids were just parasites anyway, wanting things the easy way, not willing to sweat and toil for it.

The Story
Continues in

**Touching Other Lives
Volume 3**

**Touching Other Lives
Volume 4**

Also by Margaret Gregory

<u>TYMOREAN TRUST SERIES</u>: (Fantasy)
Book 1 - Power Rising
Book 2 - Great Ones
Book 3 - The Return to Earth
Book 4 – Earth Mission
Book 5 – Alien Contact
Book 6 - Invasion
<u>ATAPI SORCERESS SERIES</u>: (Fantasy)
Prequel – Korvu: The Beginning
Book 1- The Wild One
Book 2 – Atapi Sorceress
<u>THE THIRD GENERATION SERIES</u>:(Fantasy)
Book 1 - Wanda: From Bad to Worse
Book 2 - Wanda: Choosing Crime
Wanda – Early Days (anthology) Book 1 and 2
Book 3 – Wanda: Risking Life to Live
Book 4 – Erin: The Forcing of Wisdom
Book 5 – Wanda: A New Life Part 1 – Hidden Secrets
Book 6 – Wanda: A New Life Part 2 – First Mission
Book 7 – Wanda: Full Circle
The Serpent's Shadow
Royal Favour
Foreign Agent - Thief
Prisoner - Spy

<u>HOLDER OF SECRETS SERIES</u>:
Unregarded
Unsuspected
Unrepentant

<u>STAND ALONE</u>
The Magpie's Daughter
The Chance to be Me
Maeven: Dragon Thief